D0871740

A BRILLIANT DECEPTION

Other books by Kathleen Fuller:

Santa Fe Sunrise
Special Assignment
San Antonio Sunset
San Francisco Serenade

A BRILLIANT DECEPTION

•

Kathleen Fuller

AVALON BOOKS
NEW YORK

Published by Thomas Bouregy & Co., Inc.
160 Madison Avenue, New York, NY 10016

Library of Congress Cataloging-in-Publication Data

Fuller, Kathleen.
A brilliant deception / Kathleen Fuller.
p. cm.
ISBN 978-0-8034-9877-8 (acid-free paper)
I. Title.

PS3606.U553B75 2008
813'.6—dc22
2007024157

PRINTED IN THE UNITED STATES OF AMERICA
ON ACID-FREE PAPER
BY HADDON CRAFTSMEN, BLOOMSBURG, PENNSYLVANIA

To Barbara Satow. You're simply brilliant!

Chapter One

London
April, 1810

"Another robbery!" Lily Breckenridge smoothed the wrinkled page of the newspaper and inspected the article more closely. "How intriguing."

"Only you would think a rash of robberies is intriguing." Her friend, Emily Dymoke, held up a pale blue ball gown and showed it to Lily. "What do you think?"

"I think the Bow Street Runners have failed miserably in apprehending the perpetrator," Lily replied, still perusing the article. When Emily didn't comment Lily peeked over the top edge of the newsprint. "Oh, you mean the gown." She gave it an appreciative glance. "It is lovely. And I am sure it simply looks divine on you."

Emily frowned doubtfully. "I would not say divine.

That word is usually reserved for my sister." She turned to hang the dress back in her wardrobe. "A gown looks 'divine' on Diana. On me it is merely . . . serviceable."

"Hardly, Emily." Lily thought about her own gown, an exquisite creation her mother had selected a little over a week ago. Despite its beauty, Lily would be surprised if she managed to look as "serviceable" as Emily.

She watched from the corner of Emily's bedroom as the young woman put her gown away, and tried to stem the twinge of jealousy she felt over Emily's curvy figure and petite height. True, her sister, Diana, was arguably the most beautiful woman among the peerage, but Emily, with her thick blond hair and delicate features, more than held her own.

Lily tamped down her envy. She had spent her entire life trying to accept the fact that she was an ugly duckling amidst dozens of beautiful swans. Living in a society that valued attractiveness as much as it valued money had been difficult, especially when she had entered her first Season two years ago.

"So what do you plan to wear to the cotillion?" Emily asked, fortunately interrupting Lily's train of thought. She picked up a pair of delicate slippers and examined the ribbons attached to them.

"Some dress Mother ordered for me. I have not looked at it yet. I am sure it will be fine."

Surprise registered on Emily's face. "Your mother chooses your wardrobe? I had no idea."

"She says I have no sense of style or colors."

"If it is anything like your court dress, then it will be smashing."

"Well, I do know it won't be that fancy, thank goodness. Being in that elaborate frock was nearly as unbearable as court presentation itself." Lily turned her attention back to the paper, which was infinitely more interesting than the topic of fashion. "So, who do you think is robbing the *ton* of their jewels?"

Emily crossed the room and sat on the edge of her bed next to Lily. "I have not a clue." She read over Lily's shoulder. "I just hope we do not become victims of the miscreant."

"Or miscreants. What if there are two thieves working in concert?" She looked at Emily. "One is probably the lookout while the other is sneaking inside the houses . . . but then how is he getting past the footman?" Her eyes grew wide as she fathomed the possibilities. "Or maybe he isn't a *he* at all, but a she—"

"Lily, please, you are making my head swim. Do not tell me you are planning to turn amateur detective."

"I would if I could, believe me. It would be a much more interesting endeavor than pricking my finger doing needlepoint and attending dull balls."

Emily giggled. "The last two have been frightfully boring, have they not? Please tell me the rest of the Season will be more exciting. From what Diana says there's a glorious time to be had." She lowered her voice conspiratorially. "But I seriously question my sister's interpretation of a good time, for she thought her presentation at court was brilliant, while I had to force myself to stay awake."

Lily toyed with the idea of telling Emily the truth, having been through one disastrous Season herself. But she was loath to dampen her friend's enthusiasm for her debut into London society. "I am sure you will enjoy yourself."

"Really? I certainly hope so."

For a brief moment, Lily wished she could share Emily's excitement, however, she couldn't. In fact, she was dreading the Season. It had taken her months before she could think about donning a ball gown again without her stomach turning inside out. As the only daughter of the Duke and Duchess of Breckenridge, her debut Season should have been perfect. She was well aware of the generous dowry her father offered for her future husband. She should have had her pick of eligible gentlemen, begging her to write their names on her dance card, or offering to pay her a call.

Instead she had spent her first Season blending into the wallpaper. Oh, there were a few gentlemen at the first ball who had asked her to dance. Not wanting to appear rude, she had always agreed, despite knowing that at six feet tall and willowy thin, she towered over all the women and nearly all the men in the room. And she wasn't the only one who was uncomfortable as she danced with men whose heads barely reached her shoulder.

She had felt freakish, which in turn made her incredibly self-conscious. Until she had met George. . . .

Quickly she gave herself a mental shake, shoving him from her thoughts. He was the last person she wanted to think about right now.

Lily regarded her friend again. Emily would not have the same problems. She was what a man wanted, a small woman with voluptuous curves, someone he could hold in his arms and not sprain his neck trying to look up at her.

Emily clasped Lily's large hand in her dainty one. "I am so glad we've become friends. It is hard to believe we just met a couple weeks ago at court. I feel like I've known you forever." She smiled a sweet, genuine smile.

"So do I." Her words were the truth. She had known from the start of their first conversation that she and Emily would be lifelong companions. They both had a heart for charity work. Lily had already told her about the care packages she frequently sent to the local orphanages. It was something she hadn't told anyone else, but she felt she could trust Emily. To her delight her friend had expressed enthusiasm over helping her prepare the next ones.

A touch of sadness suddenly shadowed her thoughts. Here they were talking about balls and fancy dresses that cost a fortune, while children were spending hour upon endless hour working in the factories, as chimney sweeps or other difficult, more dangerous jobs. At least she and Emily could bring them a bit of comfort for a short period of time. But Lily wished they could do more.

Lily gave Emily's hand a squeeze and then released it.

Rising, she smoothed the skirt of the light green dress her mother had suggested she wear earlier that day. "As much as I'd like to stay, it grows late, and I really must be off. I am sure Mother and Father are wondering at my delay. And I have no doubt that Hannah is bored stiff waiting for me in your kitchen." Hannah had been her maid for the past four years, and the energetic young woman simply hated being without something to do.

"I am not sure about that, Lily," Emily said, her lips twitching with a small smile. "I believe she has become, shall I say, quite smitten with our house boy."

"Trevor?" Lily's eyes grew wide with surprise as the image the Dymokes' tall, thin servant with a bright shock of red hair came into her mind. "But she has never mentioned anything regarding him before."

"Perhaps she wants to keep her feelings a secret."

"Then how do *you* know about them?"

Emily laughed. "I have my ways." At Lily's overarching look, she added, "Our cook is not the most discrete of souls, bless her heart. I have heard her more than once remark on Trevor's spoony behavior after your last visit. Truly, she says she could barely get him to resume his duties, he became so distracted."

Lily grinned. "Well, jolly good for her. Hannah is a sweet girl."

"And Trevor a fine catch—he shan't be our house boy for long, I am sure of that. There has been talk of promoting him to take charge of our stables at our country estate." They headed downstairs. "I will have Blevins bring round the carriage. It is not proper for you both to walk home at this hour, especially without an escort."

Although she lived only a few houses away in Grosvenor Square, Lily agreed. "Thank you."

"I shall return shortly."

While Emily went off to arrange the transport, Lily looked around the foyer of the Dymoke home. It was smaller than her home at Stratsford Hall, but tastefully decorated. This was Lily's second visit, the first having taken place last year when the Dymokes had thrown a lavish ball to end the London Season. She had reluctantly attended, but hadn't stayed for too long, a sudden onslaught of a headache forcing her to beg off early, before she had been formally introduced to her host, Colin Dymoke, Baron Chesreton.

She had only seen the man from afar, at a couple of parties she had attended early in the Season. He was strikingly handsome, the masculine counterpart to his gorgeous sister Diana. And from all accounts he was filled to the brim with charm. He had a reputation as a ladies' man as well, but Lily didn't pay too much attention to such gossip, and she didn't pay him much heed either. She knew such delightfully fine-looking men never noticed women like her. Not when there were so many lovely ingénues vying for their attention.

Her ears perked up at the sound of the front door opening. The Dymokes' stately butler, Blevins, instantly appeared, casting a cursory glance in her direction as he passed her by. Lily felt a cool draft of air waft into the room and heard the loud click of a door being shut.

"Lord Chesreton!" The butler exclaimed in obvious surprise. "My lady wasn't expecting you home until tomorrow."

Colin entered the foyer, removed his hat and handed it to the butler. "I returned from my trip early," he replied.

"And how were the Highlands, my lord?"

"Gorgeous. Simply gorgeous. I should like to visit again in the near future."

"I believe your mother would prefer you stay here for a good while, my lord. My lady seems much calmer when you are around."

"You don't say. I suppose she's in a tizzy over something or other?"

"I am afraid I cannot comment on that, sir. I am not privy to her tizzies."

Colin laughed. "I suppose you are not. Well, I am here to assure her that I am safe and sound."

"She'll be most happy to hear that, my lord."

Up to this point Lily had quietly observed the conversation, the profiles of the two men obscured by the shadows in the foyer. Then Colin stepped into the hall, the butler close at his heels. Her eyes met Colin's and suddenly her body swayed.

Gripping the polished wood banister for support, she tried to stem her wonder. She had thought the man was handsome from across a crowded room, but up close, he was no less than devastating. His blond hair was thick and wavy. His nose was perfectly sloped, his lips full and sensuous. But his eyes nearly undid her on the spot. Darker than perfect sapphires, they were quite literally the most gorgeous pair of eyes she had ever seen.

He tilted his head slightly, eyeing her with curiosity. "Miss?" he spoke, taking a long step toward her. His voice was deep and smooth, like honey flowing over glass. "Are you all right?"

It was at that moment she realized how tall he was. They were mere steps away from each other, and she noted he was at eye level with her. Now this was a man she could dance with. Her heartbeat accelerated at the thought of being in his arms, waltzing effortlessly around the ballroom floor. . . .

"Miss?" he said, more sternly now. "I say, are you ill? You appear flushed."

Lily made a move toward him, but caught the toe of her slipper on the hem of her dress. Robbed of her balance, she was powerless to keep her body from pitching forward.

And from falling right into Colin Dymoke's arms.

Chapter Two

"Mind your—"

Colin's warning was abruptly cut off as the young woman fell toward him. Instinctively he reached out and grabbed her around her waist. It surprised him to discover how tiny it was. She was thin, almost painfully so, and he could feel the sharp angles of her body as she leaned against him to regain her balance.

He looked at her face, which was now inches from his own. Pale skin, thin lips, sharp cheekbones. By far the tallest woman he had ever seen. Yet, he thought, as his gaze met hers fleetingly, the color of her eyes was interesting. They were a deep dark brown, nearly black, the same hue as her hair. He had the sudden sensation that he'd seen her somewhere before, probably at one of the many social events he had attended last Season.

Her cheeks, which had been rosy moments ago, now

practically glowed red. She twisted out of his grasp and stepped back, almost losing her balance a second time as her foot collided with the bottom stair.

Just then Blevins appeared at her side. "My lady, are you all right?" Concern colored his voice. "You've not injured yourself, have you?"

"No, no," she said, her gaze focused downward as she brushed her hands against the folds of her dress. "I am fine, truly."

Blevins' relief was evident. "Thank goodness, my lady. What a fortunate happenstance that my lord was here to catch your fall."

Despite her obvious embarrassment, she still lifted her chin and gave him a tight smile. Colin admired the way she held herself together.

"The carriage is on its way," Emily said, entering the room.

Colin's attention turned to his younger sister, whose sparkling blue eyes lit up with delight when she saw him.

"Colin!" she exclaimed, then hurried across the hall to greet him. Never stingy with her affections, she immediately wrapped her arms around him and hugged him tight. Then she took a step back and proceeded to take him down a peg.

"How grand of you to grace us with your presence."

"Now, Emily, do not start—"

"We never see you anymore since you've decided to travel the world." She looked up at him, her expression filled with so much righteous indignation that Colin had to bite the inside of his bottom lip to keep from grinning.

He knew from past experience to maintain perfect decorum when Emily's sensibilities were piqued.

He cast a quick glance to the woman still standing by the staircase. She was engrossed in examining the mundane finial on the end of the banister while Emily continued her lecture. "If you insist on dressing me down in front of our guest, *little sister,*" he interjected, "the least you could do is introduce me to her."

Emily's mouth formed a small *o* shape, all traces of her earlier reproach disintegrating. Her reaction was exactly as Colin had surmised. How gratifying to know he could still read her like an open book.

She turned to the woman. "Please forgive me. I've been incredibly rude. Lily, may I present you to my brother Colin Dymoke, Lord Chesreton. Colin, this is my friend, Lady Lily Thornton, daughter of the Duke of Breckenridge."

Recognition dawned as he tipped his head in deference. Now he remembered seeing her at two of the balls he'd attended last Season. The first had been the Balcarris' fete, which was thrown by his mother's longtime friend, the Countess of Hathery. The second had been at his own family's ball.

He remembered witnessing Lily dancing a minuet with an unfortunate man of short stature. The woman's reaction to her partner at the time was an exact replica to the unease she displayed now.

"I am honored to meet you," Colin said, hoping to put her at ease a bit. "But if you ladies will excuse me, I must beg your leave now." He turned to Blevins, who had remained silent since Emily entered the room. "If you would be so good as to tell me where I can find Mother?"

"She is in her sitting room with Miss Dymoke," the butler replied crisply. "Shall I announce you?"

"No, let me surprise her."

"She will probably faint dead away from shock," Emily muttered.

This time Colin couldn't help but crack a smile before heading to the drawing room.

Lily had never been so embarrassed in her entire life.

It was one thing to trip over one's overly large feet, but to then fall directly into the arms of the most handsome man in London—no, surely in all of England—was quite another.

She quickly reigned in her thoughts. It didn't matter if Colin was the most handsome fellow in the entire British Empire—and she had to believe he was somewhere among the top five—she had other things to think about.

As she entered her carriage and left for home, she sent all ruminations of Colin Dymoke away. She glanced at Hannah, who was seated directly across from her. Armed with the information Emily had revealed, she scrutinized her maid, seeking any affirmation as to what her friend said was true. Hannah was skilled in hiding her thoughts and emotions, her face often fixed in a placid visage. But even in the dim light of the carriage, Lily detected a sparkle in the woman's brown eyes, and it was clear that she was lost in her own thoughts, which were probably consumed with Trevor. Lily hid a smile, then turned her own musings to the rash of robberies taking place among the peerage. Four bracelets had been pilfered already, and it was only the beginning of the Season. The thefts had all taken place during social events, this latest one at the London estate of Lord Merriweather.

Lily tapped her chin with her gloved hand, and wondered again about the thief's motive and opportunity. *Or thieves.* The entire thing was most fascinating. However, she did hope the perpetrator would be caught, and soon. It just didn't do for a criminal to be running rampant through the *ton.*

"Honestly, Colin, I am at a loss as to why you feel you must be out of the country all the time. Even when you are here you forget about your poor, neglected mother." Elizabeth Dymoke folded her small hands in her lap. "Now that you've taken to gallivanting all over creation, you seem to think being with your family isn't worth your time anymore."

He fought the urge to roll his eyes. "I am here now, Mother," he said, crossing the room and planting a kiss on her cheek. She and his sister Diana sat in their usual chairs next to the window and opposite each other in the large room. The heavy emerald-colored curtains were already drawn for the evening.

He sank into a soft, plush chair directly across from them and crossed his ankle over his knee. "Aren't you going to ask me about my trip?"

"Let me guess," Diana said. "It was marvelous, and you hope to go again in the future. Does that about cover it?"

"You know me too well," he mumbled. "Thank you for taking all the fun out of it."

Elizabeth rose from her seat, crossed the room and rang the bell for a servant. Immediately Blevins appeared.

"Tell Cook we will take our supper here. I will also have a cup of tea." She looked to Colin.

He stood. "I must decline, I am afraid. I still have not unpacked." But the glare his mother tossed him had him sitting back down. He should have known she would not have let him go so easily.

"Colin will be staying for supper, Blevins." She visually pinned him in his seat. "Now, what would you like to drink, dear?"

"A brandy for me, if you please," he replied meekly.

"Diana?" Elizabeth asked.

His sister looked up from her needlework. "Nothing for me, Mother. I am neither thirsty nor hungry."

Elizabeth frowned at her eldest daughter. "You must have at least a scone, or perhaps a couple of those ginger biscuits you are so fond of."

Diana shook her head, sighing softly. "Truly, Mama, I am not hungry." Exasperation filled her round, expressive eyes; eyes that for the past two Seasons had every eligible gentleman in the *ton* offering marriage, and several ineligible ones offering indecent proposals. Fortunately for Colin she had made quick work of those bounders, or else it could have been pistols at dawn, for he'd defend her honor without hesitation, and Emily's as well.

"I had a large meal at lunch," Diana continued, explaining her case. "Harriet and I dined at Lady Myerson's. It was quite extravagant and I simply could not offend Harriet's aunt by refusing the second helpings she offered. So I honestly cannot partake of another bite of food."

Elizabeth glanced at Diana, scanning her slender frame. "I am inclined to disbelieve you, for you rarely eat enough to keep a bird alive when you dine at home."

"Lady Myerson has an exceptional cook."

"And you are implying that our Isabel is not?"

Colin chuckled. "I do not think she is implying anything, Mother. I think she is quite clear on the subject."

Diana gave Colin a brilliant smile. "As usual, Colin understands me perfectly," she said.

"Hmmph." Their mother sat back down in her chair. "It is no wonder the two of you are not married off. You both are most contrary."

With a flick of her delicate wrist, Diana waved off her mother's comment. "How can you expect me to decide on a husband so soon? You've seen all the cards I've received. There are so many men to choose from."

"And you say that with such humility," Colin quipped.

Diana gave him a fairly sour look. "And you . . . well, I am not sure what you are about. Half the women in London have been asking about you, wanting to know when you were returning. Carolina Derry has been most persistent. Even a bit bold, if I do say so. She seems quite smitten with you."

Colin nodded. He knew Carolina had been interested in him for the past two Seasons now. She was a beautiful young woman, but she didn't really strike a chord within him. He found her a tad vain and rather boring.

"I daresay her mother already has her trousseau picked out," Diana continued, her lips forming a teasing smile.

"You can be sure that I am not in any hurry to be leg-shackled to some bird-witted female."

"Not all of the ingénues are bird-witted," Elizabeth said at the precise moment Emily entered the room.

Colin got up from his seat. "I beg to differ, Mother, for here is an example of one now."

Emily, who had heard his words and her mother's previous ones, gave him a sharp punch in the arm. "At least I am not a jingle-brain."

"Enough!" Elizabeth brought her fingertips to her temples and closed her blue eyes. "I must insist you all behave like adults, or I shall send the lot of you back to the nursery."

"Does that mean you will hire a new governess for me?" Colin wiggled his eyebrows devilishly.

At that moment the butler entered the room with their drinks. Lady Chesreton opened her eyes. "Ah, Blevins, my tea," she said, casting an annoyed glance at her children. "And just in the nick of time."

Colin accepted the brandy from Blevins' out-stretched hand. He took a sip and let the burning liquid slide down his throat. Swirling the amber-colored beverage in his glass, he watched the women as they settled to dine. A warm feeling flowed through him, and not because of the brandy. He loved his family, and tonight's joviality reminded him of times long ago, before his father had died.

"Colin, come get something to eat," his mother called from the sideboard at the front of the room. "And convince Diana to join us as well, or she shall end up resembling that poor creature Lily Breckenridge."

"Mother!" Emily said, holding two ginger biscuits directly over a small plate. "How can you say something so insensitive?"

"I meant no harm, Emily. Lily is a lovely young lady . . . on the inside." Emily began to protest but Elizabeth cut her off. "Do not misunderstand me. I merely meant that she is too thin, and a trifle bit too tall."

"A trifle?" Diana asked, still firmly planted in her chair. Colin knew it would take an act of God to move her from her position, now that her mind was settled on not eating. "That is like saying that the Marquess of Bondelely is a trifle bit too short."

Colin chuckled. The Marquess was short to the extreme. "Now *they* would make an intriguing couple," he couldn't resist saying.

The sound of a plate being slammed against the sideboard abruptly ended his humor. Biscuits littered the floor around Emily's feet. She clenched her fists at her sides.

"I am appalled that you would joke at Lily's expense, and only moments after she has left our home." Her voice sounded shaky, and her eyes grew moist. She glared at Colin and Diana. "Not everyone can be as beautiful as you two."

"Emily, calm down. We were only teasing," Colin said.

"You were not teasing. You were being cruel." She jerked her arm away from his. "Lily cannot help her height. God created her that way, and it is exceedingly awful of you to mock her for it." Emily turned to her mother. "I will retire to my room for the night, Mother. I have suddenly lost my appetite." Before anyone could utter a sound she dashed out of the room.

"Well, Colin. That was poorly done."

"Me?" He looked at Diana. "You were the one who compared Lily to Bondelely."

"You were the one who laughed!"

Elizabeth picked up the bell and gave it a hard shake. Within seconds the butler appeared.

"Blevins," she said wearily. "I believe I am in need of another tea."

Chapter Three

Lily brought her gloved fingertips to her lips, trying to stifle the yawn that was threatening to escape. She cast a glance at her mother, who was standing a few feet away. The woman was so thoroughly engaged in a lively conversation with Lady Thewlis she didn't seem to notice her daughter was beyond bored.

Lily glanced around the drawing room. The cotillion had drawn a small crowd, mostly due to the exclusive guest list of Lady Thewlis and her husband, Sir Andrew Bettleton. Emily was here, along with Diana and their mother. And Colin. Lily tried not to look in his direction, but she could hardly help it. Unfortunately she had been witness to him dancing with Carolina Derry, and she had to admit they looked good together. She was very pretty, with cascading curls of chestnut hair, slight of build but still curvy in all the right places, and an ivory complexion that she never failed to accentuate with her choices of lovely gowns and dresses. Lily found herself watching them, trying to stem the bitter feelings threatening to envelope her. As the two of them glided across the floor she couldn't help but wish she were the one dancing with him. It was a preposterous and futile thought, but one she couldn't completely dispel.

Now he was standing across the room near his family, speaking with two other gentlemen. He looked splendid in his dark suit, the cut accentuating his finest features— his broad shoulders, tapered waist, and long legs. She didn't want to dwell on those features for any length of time. Her hand went to her heated cheek. *Too late.*

Averting her eyes, she looked at the entrance of the room just in time to see two fellows stroll in. Her heart sank to her knees as George Clayburn, the seventh Baronet of Brightonham—which was hardly a title at all, she thought sourly—entered the party. Mere seconds passed before his gaze matched hers. It was almost as if he'd been seeking her out.

Drat. The scoundrel had seen her. Frantically she looked around, searching for someplace to escape or hide from her former betrothed. To her dismay there wasn't a potted plant in sight, and she appeared to be surrounded by the most diminutive members of the *ton.* Hastily she abandoned her mother, who seemed to have forgotten about her, and retreated to Emily and the rest of the Dymoke clan. At least there was safety in numbers.

Unfortunately George appeared to be headed in the same direction.

Dread pooled in her belly, as it always did when she saw—or thought—of George. Nearly a year had passed since their broken engagement, but he could still make her feel more insecure and unattractive than she normally did at these types of events.

The quartet that had been taking an overly long break chose that exact moment to begin playing again. Just as Lily reached Emily, a young gentleman asked her friend to dance. Diana was already circling the ballroom floor with another one of her handsome partners. Which left Lily standing next to Colin and his two friends, feeling more exposed than ever.

"We've just learned of a positively brilliant gaming establishment," one of the gentlemen said.

The other one added, "A place where one is guaranteed to win."

"You know I do not gamble," Colin said. "Why would I be interested in such a place?"

Lily began inching away from the men. Obviously they hadn't noticed her yet.

"Pish-posh, Colin, do not be such a dullard." This came from one of the gentlemen.

"I will admit to indulging every once in a while," the third man said.

Lily recognized his voice and realized it belonged to Gavin Parringer, who was a marquess or an earl or some such thing, but she really couldn't think straight because George was quickly closing the gap between them.

"So exactly where is this supposed wonderful place?"

Colin asked, although he didn't sound terribly intrigued. Lily surmised he was just being polite.

"Seven Dials," the other man said.

Colin inhaled a sharp breath. "There's nothing brilliant about *that* part of the city."

Lily could barely hear the conversation now. She turned and started to walk away, which is what she should have done the minute Emily and Diana stepped their dainty slippers onto the dance floor.

"Lady Lily, surely you aren't leaving on my account?" George's caustic question burned her ears.

She bit the inside of her lip and slowly turned around. Colin, Gavin, and the other nameless man were eyeing her curiously. Naturally they would choose that moment to finally realize she was there.

Oh, Lord, why is this happening to me?

"Not at all, Sir Clayburn," she managed, thankful her steady voice wasn't echoing her quaking insides. "I am merely thirsty, and I thought I'd try a glass of Lady Thewlis' lemonade." She was almost an inch taller than him, but she still felt dwarfed by his oily presence. Still, she had to admit he was handsomer than most men. His looks had been what drew her to him in the first place. That and his charm, which he was seriously lacking at the moment.

"Of course," George said, edging closer to her. "You do not do much more than drink lemonade and taste the crudités at these events, do you Lady Lily?"

An unpleasant shiver coursed through her. "I—I do not know what you mean."

"Come now. Surely you can see nearly all the ladies are out on the ballroom floor, dancing with their partners. And here you are, standing next to three obviously available gentlemen. Why, they have not noticed you at all."

Lily's mouth went dry. Her heart, which was previously at her knees, plunged clear to her toes. It was an insult. Not a direct smear on her reputation or her person, but a pointed insult nevertheless. One that made her wish she could disappear into the wainscoting behind her.

Instead she did the next best thing. She fled.

Tears nearly blinded her as she entered the foyer. "My cloak," she said curtly to the footman near the front door. As she waited for him to comply, she gave herself a thorough mental scolding. *Why do I let him get to me so? He is a blighter and an ingrate and not worth it—*

"Lady Lily?"

Whirling around, her eyes widened as she realized who stood behind her. Colin Dymoke was the last person she had expected to see. Or wanted to see. "Go away." She sounded like a four-year-old child on the verge of a tantrum, but at that moment she really didn't care.

"I do not believe I will." He stepped toward her, his tone soft and low. "Are you all right?"

"Of course I am." She resisted the urge to sniff. "I am fine. I have a splitting headache, so if you'll take your leave please—"

"Your cloak, my lady."

Colin intercepted the garment from the footman before Lily could say a word. "Allow me." He held it out toward her.

Lily studied him for a moment. She had already embarrassed herself once in his presence, back at the Dymoke home. Now she had been humiliated a second time, but yet here he was, checking on her welfare and even assisting her with her cloak. Why would he even bother?

"I've been robbed!" a woman suddenly shrieked from the ballroom.

Lily froze. Robbed?

"My bracelet! My diamond and ruby bracelet. It is missing!"

She felt the weight of her evening cloak on her shoulders as Colin draped it around her. At the same time she heard something drop near her slipper.

She and Colin both looked down.

There, twinkling in the low light of the lit tapers that illuminated the foyer, lying on the marble tile next to her robin's egg blue slippers that her mother insisted she had to wear to the cotillion that evening, was a bracelet.

A ruby and diamond bracelet.

Chapter Four

Colin stared at the glittering jewels resting on the floor near Lily's foot. He blinked. Twice. He still saw the bracelet, proving he wasn't imagining things.

"Andrew, I've been *violated*!" Lady Thewlis' normally high-pitched voice reached a new octave as she continued to fret about her stolen jewelry. Colin heard the soothing tones of Sir Andrew consoling her, along with the collective gasps and comments of the rest of the guests in the ballroom.

"I daresay the Bracelet Bandit has struck again!"

"Right under our very noses!"

"He's a most crafty fellow, is he not?"

Colin looked at Lily. Her brown eyes were at least twice their normal size, and her complexion had turned a rather frightful shade of gray.

She knelt down to retrieve the bracelet. But before

26

she could grasp it, he swooped in and whisked it off the floor. The commotion in the next room continued while he contemplated what to do. Never in his wildest imaginings would he have thought the Duke of Breckenridge's daughter a thief. Yet stranger things had happened among the peerage. The fact that the offspring of one of the wealthiest members of the *ton* had sticky fingers shouldn't have come as that much of a surprise.

But it did. And he wasn't positive that the odd expression on her face was actually guilt at being caught red-handed.

"M-my lord," she said, her voice trembling. "I-I have no idea how that . . . how the bracelet—"

"Search the premises!" Sir Andrew's bellow resounded through the front hall.

Colin reacted quickly. "Stay here," he ordered, pinning Lily in place with his gaze. "I will be right back."

She nodded as he dashed into the ballroom.

"I've found it!" he called out, holding the bracelet aloft. He threaded his way through the milling crowd to Lady Thewlis. He bowed before handing her the jeweled piece. "The clasp must have broken, my lady. Perhaps your jeweler should take a look at it."

"Thank you so much, Lord Chesreton." Lady Thewlis gratefully accepted the bracelet and inspected it closely. "The clasp seems to be intact, but I will take it to my jeweler posthaste." She let out a nervous chuckle. "Thank goodness this was a false alarm. For a moment I thought I had been a victim of that dreadful bandit."

"A natural reaction, considering the circumstances."

Colin glanced over his shoulder to see if Lily was still in the foyer. She wasn't. He groaned inwardly. "Begging your leave, my lady," he said, backing away from Lady Thewlis. "I shall depart and allow you to enjoy the rest of your evening."

"Much obliged, Chesreton." Sir Andrew clasped his beefy hand around Colin's and shook it heartily. "You've saved the day, mate."

Colin acknowledged him with a hurried nod, then spun on his heel and exited the room just in time to see the door to the front entrance close. Without retrieving his overcoat, he chased after Lily. The woman wasn't going to escape that easily.

Lily's heart pounded in her chest with such force she thought it might explode. How had Lady Thewlis' bracelet ended up in her cloak pocket? Surely some kind of mix-up had occurred, although she couldn't fathom what it could be. However, that had to be the only explanation for why some other woman's jewelry had ended up in her possession.

The image of Colin's stunned expression, followed by his accusing glare flitted through her mind. The cad had actually thought she had stolen the bracelet! The unmitigated gall of the man. He had judged and condemned her guilty in a matter of a few seconds.

Her heartbeat accelerated. First George's insult, then Colin's silent accusation. They both added up to the most dreadful night of her entire life.

As her foot landed on the carriage step, she heard him call her name.

"Lady Lily!" Colin shouted from behind her. "A word, if you please."

For a fraction of a second she considered ignoring him. But she realized selective hearing would not only be the epitome of poor manners, it would serve to make her look guiltier than she already did.

Pressing her hand against her chest to steady her heart's rhythm, she turned and faced him. "My lord," she said, forcing a tight smile. "I was just leaving."

"I can see that." He stopped directly in front of her. "I believe I requested you remain in the Thewlis' foyer."

"Yes, well—"

"You deliberately defied me."

His choice of words pricked at her. "Defied you? Lord Chesreton, I believe I am free to leave a party if I desire to do so."

"Not after you have relieved the hostess of her jewelry!"

Lily quickly moved away from the carriage, not wanting her driver to hear the accusations. Colin followed closely behind. Lily turned and spoke in a low voice. "I did no such thing!"

"Then you can explain how Lady Thewlis' bracelet found its way into your possession?"

"I—I . . ." Lily pressed her lips together. How could she explain the inexplicable? And how could she even *think* clearly with him standing in front of her, his finely featured countenance not the least bit diminished in the pale yellow glow of the street gaslight. It was downright criminal to be that exceptional looking.

She fought to gather her wits. For one thing, she was innocent. For another thing, Colin was just a man, albeit a well put together one. But a man nevertheless, and he certainly wasn't her judge. "My lord, it is true I cannot explain why the bracelet was in my cloak. But what motive do I have? I own many bracelets, all bought and paid for." She lifted her left hand and exposed three strands of jewels circling her wrist. The sapphires, diamonds, pearls and emeralds glittered in their gold settings under the lamplight.

He seemed to consider her words for a moment, his gaze fixated on the bracelets. "Perhaps boredom drove you to it," he posited, although he sounded much less sure than before. "Or possibly you possess uncontrollable envy over the jewelry. Or maybe—"

"This is ridiculous. I will not stand here and have you denigrate my character in this fashion. If you are so inclined to believe me a thief, then why did you protect me? Why not expose me for the wicked criminal you seem to think I am?"

He glowered. "Sarcasm does not become you, my lady."

"And neither does patience. So unless you plan to drag me to the nearest constable, I am taking my leave. Now." Tugging her cloak closer to her body, she turned to her driver. "James, take me home." She walked to her carriage and took the large man's hand.

"One more thing, Lady Lily," Colin said.

"What is it now?" she said, whirling around.

He stepped toward her, decreasing the space between them. "You are a friend of my sister Emily," he said quietly, but with extreme seriousness. "A dear friend, from what I can gather. It was for her sake I didn't expose you tonight. That, and the hope this indiscretion will be a one-time event." His blue eyes turned colder than ice. "But be aware, my lady. Next time I will not be so charitable. I will turn you in without a moment's hesitation." He turned his back to her and walked back into the Thewlis' house.

Fuming, Lily entered the carriage and plopped down on the velvet cushioned seat. "How dare he?" she said aloud as James shut the door. "How dare he accuse me and threaten me in the same breath?"

As her carriage pulled away her anger subsided, replaced by a sickening feeling inside. Regardless of her innocence and Colin Dymoke's impertinence, one fact did remain: The bracelet had been in her pocket. And somehow she had to find out how it had gotten there.

Chapter Five

"**O**h darling, do hurry," the duchess urged as she breezed into Lily's private dressing room. "Our coach will be ready at any moment. We mustn't be late for the Balcarris' ball." Lady Breckenridge's anxious features softened as she walked over to her daughter. She laid her hand on Lily's shoulder. "You look lovely, dear."

Lily regarded her reflection in the gilded mirror. Hannah had curled her hair into soft ringlets around her face, but the curls were already drooping. A sparkling emerald and ruby choker adorned her neck, her mother's selection, of course. The vibrant tone of the jewels only intensified her pallid skin tone.

She did *not* want to go to this party.

"I believe you will catch the eye of many a gentleman tonight," her mother said with an encouraging smile.

Lily returned it with a wan smile of her own. Moments like these intensified her feeling that she was a disappointment to her parents. Livinia had been a diamond of the first water back in her day, easily catching the eye of the dashing Trevor, Duke of Breckenridge. Even now her mother and father were still the toast of the senior members of the peerage, and both had aged most gracefully. But for some inexplicable reason they had spawned a daughter who was freakishly tall and much too thin, an aberration among the stringent standard of beauty their society held.

Apparently noticing her daughter's lack of enthusiasm, Livinia frowned. "Is something amiss, dear? You seem a bit out of sorts tonight."

It would take Lily hours to detail everything that was wrong. She also didn't want her mother to worry, so she covered the truth. "No, Mother. I am fine. Everything is as neat as nine pence."

Relief washed over Lady Breckenridge's face. "Thank goodness. It simply would not do for your father and I to explain your absence to Lady Hathery, as this is one of the most important parties of the Season." Her mother placed a finger under Lily's chin and gently tilted her face toward her. "I know this Season has been especially difficult for you, what with all that ugliness with George."

Lily nodded, but didn't elaborate on her mother's comment. Her parents didn't know the real story behind Lily breaking her betrothal to George, and she would keep it that way. It had been painful enough with only the two of them knowing what really happened. To divulge it further to anyone else, even her mother and father, would be beyond excruciating.

Unfortunately George was the least of her problems at the moment. Without a doubt he would be there, but he wasn't the person she most wanted to avoid.

That honor went to Colin Dymoke.

She wasn't in the mood to be called a thief all over again. And she was nearly positive he would also be in attendance tonight, considering the close friendship between his family and the Balcarris' was well known throughout the *ton*.

Her mother lowered her hand and sighed. "You are the light of our lives, darling. All your father and I want is for you to be happy."

Lily's tension ebbed slightly at her mother's sincerity. She stood and stepped in front of her and gazed down. She was at least half a foot taller than the petite duchess. Lily's heart was filled with tremendous love for her mother, who had always encouraged her, never making her feel that she was less than everything they'd always dreamed of. "I know you do, Mama. And I thank you for not forcing me to choose another suitor. It means so much that you and Father want me to marry for love—despite how difficult that's turning out to be."

Livinia regarded her daughter for a long moment. She reached up and touched Lily's cheek. "It is the extreme folly of youth that sees only what is on the surface," she said solemnly. "You are a beautiful, intelligent woman, my darling. Do not let anyone tell you otherwise."

"I am glad you think so," Lily said, unable to keep the bitter edge out of her tone. "Of course every mother thinks her child is the loveliest."

"That's not the reason I am saying that. I say it because it is true. I also know you will find a gentleman out there who will truly appreciate you."

Lily started to protest, to say that she would not be the least bothered if she never married, but she couldn't, because it wasn't the truth. Not when it was so obvious her mother desired her daughter to be wed, and not when Lily held that desire as well, buried deep inside her heart. It was that desire that had allowed her to succumb to George so quickly, and to turn a blind eye to what should have been obvious from the start of their relationship—that he had no intention of loving her at all.

With a small smile the duchess drew away. "We should be on our way, darling. Shall we go downstairs?"

Lily nodded, then followed her mother out into the hall, struggling to stem the butterflies that suddenly appeared in her stomach. Now would be an excellent time to feign a headache, except her headache excuse was wearing rather thin lately, as she had used it to avoid two other parties earlier in the Season. Besides, she had already committed to attending this fete, and she refused to go back on her word.

Michael Balcarris, the Earl of Hathery, and his mother had thrown an exceptional party. Throughout the house vases overflowed with fresh roses, filling the rooms with their fragrant scent. Beeswax candles glowed in golden candelabras and crystal chandeliers. A small stringed quartet had been playing for the last hour, their performance impeccable. Even the lemonade the countess served was lightly sweet and very refreshing.

Lily couldn't wait to go home.

For the hundredth time since her arrival she scanned the ballroom, looking for Colin. Fortunately there was no sign of him, and George had failed to make an appearance as well. But she couldn't celebrate just yet, and she remained guarded. The night was far from over.

The musicians ended their song, and the gentlemen began to escort their partners off the floor. Lily saw Emily Dymoke approaching, her hand tucked firmly in the crook of Lord Hathery's arm.

Lily pushed her thoughts of Colin to the side for a moment. This time she was grateful for once to be standing on the sidelines. She hadn't been chosen by Lord Hathery as a dance partner this evening, and that was a good thing. A *very* good thing.

Not that the earl wasn't handsome, for he was a rather attractive man, with light brown hair and winsome green eyes. And the fact that he was only a couple of inches shorter than she made her feel less self-conscious than normal.

The earl's biggest problem was that he was a dandy of the worst sort. A fop, and occasionally a true bore. The one time he had asked her to dance, he expounded nonstop on the intricacies of creating exactly the right folds and knots in his neckcloth. By the end of the dance Lily was ready to strangle him with his own cravat.

"Ah, Lady Lily," the earl drawled as he and Emily stopped in front of her. "My, but your name is quite the tongue twister, is it not?" With an exaggerated motion he picked up his decorative quizzing glass and peered through it. "I do hope you are enjoying yourself. You would not believe the, ah, lengths that Mother and I have gone to in arranging this *fete*. We spent hours and hours of painstaking labor to achieve the perfect effect we wanted."

Courtesy precluded her from not responding, although she would rather have gone swimming in the Thames than hear about the earl and his mother's lengths. And she knew for a fact that any labor involved had been performed by the Balcarris' servants, not the soft-handed earl. "It is a splendid party, Lord Hathery," she said, determined to keep her remarks short and to the point.

Lowering his glass, he arched a delicately shaped eyebrow. "Merely splendid?" he asked, as if she had just plied him with an insult instead of a compliment. "Can you think of, um, any *other* party that has yet compared with this one? I doubt that you can."

Lily looked at Emily, who was standing beside the earl and silently mocking him, right down to his indignant eyebrow. Before Lily could stop it, a giggle escaped.

Lord Hathery immediately turned to the side. Emily, who was now the picture of composure, gazed up at him with wide-eyed innocence. She released his arm and gave him an exaggerated curtsy. "Thank you ever so much for the dance, my lord."

He looked at both women suspiciously for a moment, then spoke. "My pleasure, Miss Emily. I say, you are a most smashing dancer. Then again, you always have been." He nodded at her, then at Lily. "If you ladies will, ah, excuse me, I shall go see how Mother is faring. This entire process has been most wearing on her."

When the earl had retreated from view, Emily turned to Lily. "I say, Lord Hathery," she mimicked, catching his snooty tone to perfection. "You are, um, a most cork-brained man."

Lily couldn't help but laugh, though she knew she shouldn't. "I imagine it is not proper to make fun of our host," she said, trying to sound stern, but failing.

"Yes, I know, I know." Emily's frustration was evident. "It is most un-Christian of me, is it not? Yet I cannot help it. Michael never used to be this way. You should have known him when we were growing up. He was so witty, a brilliant conversationalist, really. And smart, much smarter than I could ever dream of being." Melancholy filled her eyes as she watched him on the opposite side of the room, standing beside his mother. "Now look at him. His clothing is outrageous—only a conceited fool would wear a corset, and I daresay he is wearing one, as stiff as his dance movements are. The only topics he converses about now are gossip and himself. Oh, Lily, he is so high in the instep as to be insufferable."

By the sadness in Emily's voice, Lily knew she wasn't simply making fun of the earl anymore. "What do you think made him change so drastically?"

"I do not know. But I cannot help but think it had something to do with his attending Oxford, for it was upon his return from university that he began acting this way." Slowly she tore her gaze from the earl. "I miss my friend," she said softly. "I cannot relate to this 'new' version of Michael Balcarris."

The musicians began playing, and once again many of the gentlemen sought out partners to dance with. A look of determination crossed Emily's features, and she adjusted her white elbow-length satin gloves. "I shall not let Michael spoil my evening," she resolved. "If he wishes to be a beef-witted, cabbage-head buzzard—"

"Emily," Lily chided.

"I know. Not very virtuous of me either." She sighed. "Believe it or not, my tongue has gotten me in trouble on more than one occasion."

Lily gave her friend an empathetic smile. For the first time this evening she started to relax. No Colin. No George. And Emily's outrageous comments had a way of making her forget her own difficulties, at least for the moment.

"I see Diana is already out there." Emily nodded toward the dance floor. "That certainly isn't a surprise."

Lily watched as Diana and her dashing partner smoothly moved around the ballroom. Diana's soft, light green gown—the color a perfect foil for her pale blond hair—accentuated her petite figure. She wore almost no jewelry, just a sparkling pair of diamond teardrop earrings that glittered in her perfectly shaped earlobes. Lily couldn't find a single flaw in her beauty. The familiar pang of envy encroached on her emotions, but she fought it back.

Lord Wattersly, who Lily and Emily had met at a dinner party last week, started toward them, an unfamiliar gentleman striding beside him. Certain that one of them wanted to dance with Emily, Lily moved away until she felt her back press against the wall. She realized her assumption was correct when both of the young men ignored her and walked directly to her friend.

"It is about time!" Emily exclaimed, at the same moment the red-haired man opened his mouth to speak, gesturing to his friend as if he were about to introduce him. Emily suddenly breezed past the stunned gentlemen, her celestial blue satin gown swirling around her ankles. "I shall have a word with him, that I will," she mumbled as she left.

Wearing dumbfounded expressions on their faces, the men looked to Lily, who could do nothing but shrug in ignorance. Her gaze followed the direction Emily had taken, but she had instantly disappeared into the milling crowd. Her friend's behavior was most curious. Lily wondered who Emily had seen to make her rush off so abruptly.

Lily looked to Lord Wattersly, who simply stared at her as if he were in contemplation about something. Then he turned to his friend, who immediately gave a quick shake of his head. Both of them walked away without saying a word.

Heat suffused her cheeks as she glanced around her, hoping none of the gossipy hens seated at the perimeter of the room saw the embarrassing interchange, or rather *lack* of interchange between her and the two men. But upon hearing the quiet snickers and muffled murmurs of the nosy women, she knew they had seen her rejection.

Quickly Lily left, weaving her way through the crowd of people who weren't currently dancing. She had to admit that this was one of the more well-attended parties she had been to all month, and it could have been slightly tolerable if she hadn't been so deliberately snubbed. This time she felt a real headache coming on, her temples pulsing with pain.

She was partway to the other side of the room when she saw him standing near the ballroom entrance. Dread traveled down her spine. His handsome face contorted in an aggravated expression as he listened to Emily, who apparently was giving him another dressing down. But Lily didn't care one whit what his sister was saying to him. She was only concerned about one thing.

Colin had decided to come after all.

Chapter Six

"Emily, you are growing tiresome." Colin scowled at his sibling. "I did not come here to receive another lecture from you."

"Why are you here at all? You are two hours late—do you know how many times Mama has asked after you?"

"What I do with myself is none of your concern. I am not a child, and you *certainly* are not my mother, so I would ask you not to behave as such."

"I cannot help that I care about you!"

"Are you not going to introduce me, Ches?" Gavin Parringer interjected.

Colin turned to his friend, Gavin, who had accompanied him to the party. They had both stopped at White's before coming here. Now he wished they'd stayed at the gentleman's club. "Sorry." With a trace of annoyance in his voice he said, "Emily, may I introduce you to Gavin Parringer, Viscount Tamesbury. Gavin, this is Miss Emily Dymoke." He let out a long suffering sigh. "My meddling sister."

"Pleasure to meet you, Miss Emily." Gavin bowed at the waist.

Emily didn't respond. She simply stared, her mouth open slightly. It was only after Colin nudged her in the side that she replied. "L-likewise," she said, a shy blush blooming on her cheeks in a most un-Emily-like way.

Colin looked from his sister to his friend, who seemed oblivious of Emily's unusual reaction to him. Indeed, he wasn't even looking at her, instead investigating the dancers and the crowd on the periphery of the ballroom floor.

"Did you have something to tell me, Emily?" Colin asked, drawing her attention away from Gavin. "Or was that charming display of pique merely for everyone else's benefit?"

That made her redden even more, and she grasped Colin by the arm, pulling him a few steps away from Gavin. "I suppose now that you are here you can make amends to Lady Lily," she said in a low, stern voice.

"The Duke of Breckenridge's daughter?" Gavin piped in, his attention fully focused back on Colin and Emily. "You have not offended *her* have you? I shudder to think of what might happen—"

"I have not offended anyone," Colin said, irked by Emily's pestering. If anything, Lily owed him an apology. And a thank-you for keeping her secret, something he still regretted. Thus far he had received neither.

Emily jabbed him in the shoulder with her fingertip. "Have you forgotten what you said about her?"

Colin raised a questioning brow.

"About who?" Gavin queried.

Awareness suddenly dawned on him. Colin had completely forgotten about the conversation he and Diana had engaged in concerning Lily. Clearly, Emily had not. "That was a bit of harmless bamming," Colin told Emily. "Besides, she was not there to hear it anyway, was she? Therefore, no harm done."

"Who wasn't there? To hear what?" Gavin twittered. "Zounds, man, you must tell me, for I am surely dying of curiosity now."

"You are worse than a gossipy hen, Gav." Colin could feel his irritation rising to epic proportions. He should have skipped the party tonight and faced his mother's censure another day. He was hardly in a good mood, spending most of last night and all of today wondering if he'd done the right thing regarding Lily and the bracelet. His thoughts had seesawed for hours. It had been dishonest of him not to say anything, and that truly bothered him.

Yet something had kept him from contacting the authorities. Despite the visual evidence to the contrary, he had a hard time believing her capable of perpetrating any crime, much less burgling something as trivial as a bracelet, considering her family's sizable wealth. And although he didn't know her very well, she had a refreshing air of sincerity and integrity about her.

However, there was one thing he knew for sure—he

did not like this struggle of conscience. Not one little bit. Which was why he wished his friend and his sister would stop adding to his consternation and simply shut up.

Emily cast a glance over her shoulder, then squeezed his arm with a bit more enthusiasm than he would have liked. "She is coming this way. You *must* ask her to dance. Right now."

"Emily—"

"Colin," Emily hissed, leaning closer to him. "She is almost here. Ask her to dance."

"I am not in the mood to dance."

"Please?"

He looked at her, not missing the pleading look in her eyes. It was genuine, just as everything about Emily was genuine. There wasn't a manipulative bone in her body, at least not one she purposely used.

Pulling on his sleeve, she drew him closer to her. "She has not danced with anyone tonight. Nor have I seen her dancing at any of the other balls we have attended this Season. She pretends it doesn't bother her, but I know it does. So would you please do this one small favor? For me?"

Colin groaned, for he could not refuse Emily when she was this benevolent. That, and he was at a loss for an excuse not to ask Lily. Even Gavin was looking at him expectantly. Tugging resignedly at the lapels of his evening coat, he tried to act at least a little interested. "All right, if it will keep you from badgering me further, I will ask her to dance."

Emily brought her gloved hands together with a muffled clap. "Excellent, Colin! You are a most gallant man, even if you are wearing a scowl that would frighten the dead. You have my deepest thanks, brother dear. I promise you will not regret this."

He peered at her beneath hooded lids, not bothering to mask the unease he felt as he saw Lady Lily approach, only to stop in her tracks and look directly at him. "We shall see about that, little sister."

Lily knew she should move, but her traitorous feet would not comply. Instead, she remained perfectly still, with the exception of a few bumps and jostles by fabulously attired party guests as they maneuvered around her. Her gaze was focused on Colin, who by the sour expression on his face looked as if he'd just been sentenced to Newgate Prison. Emily, on the other hand, clapped her hands together and looked deliriously pleased.

Standing on slightly raised tiptoes, she was able to easily see over the heads of most of the guests. Colin tugged at the lapels of his black evening coat, which looked most smashing on him. The jacket accentuated the broadness of his shoulders, a trait she found very appealing. She already knew how strong he was from their earlier encounter at Emily's house. The image of him wrapping his arm around her waist darted through her mind.

She watched as he stepped away from his sister and disappeared within the crowd. The slim fellow with the jovial countenance who had been standing next to him leaned forward and spoke to Emily. A brilliant smile lit up her face and she slid her hand through his crooked arm. They glided onto the dance floor, Emily practically beaming.

Lily thought they made a rather charming couple, and Emily certainly looked happy. Unbidden, jealousy pinched at her once again. It was most frustrating, since she always worked so hard to keep those feelings at bay while she was attending these sorts of events, and they always managed to claw their way to the surface of her consciousness. It was getting more and more difficult to quash her covetousness. Especially tonight, when she seemed to have such a tenuous hold on her emotions.

Threading her fingers tightly together, she turned her back to the dancing couples on the floor. She didn't know where Colin had gone off to and she didn't care. She now had an excellent opportunity to leave the party undetected, and she planned to take advantage of it.

The music stopped, and the couples began to flow off the dance floor. The throng of people instantly grew thick, preventing her from taking more than a couple steps at a time. More than once she felt the sharp pain of a man's dress heel press against the toe of her white slipper.

When she was almost to the door, she felt a tickle on her shoulder. She brushed it away, only to have it appear again. Puzzled, she touched her chin to the top of her shoulder to peer over her capped sleeve when she saw a man's gloved finger tap it once more, a tad more firmly this time.

"Lady Lily?"

Colin. With trepidation she turned around. His tone sounded stiff, his expression set in stone. *What does he want now? To berate me further?* Lily gave him a miniscule curtsy. "Lord Chesreton," she gritted out.

"Would, um . . ." He tugged at his cravat.

To her surprise, Lily realized he was nervous. Or at the very least uncomfortable. She tilted her head to the side and regarded him curiously.

"Would you care to dance?" he blurted out.

He couldn't have shocked her more if he had said he'd just been crowned the King of France. In fact, Colin Dymoke being the King of France seemed more believable than him actually wanting to dance with her.

"Lady Lily? Did you hear me?"

"Dance?"

"Yes, dance. You know . . . a waltz, or a minuet. I assume you know how to dance?"

"Of course I know to dance," she exclaimed. "As a matter of fact, I adore dancing. I am a very good dancer." At least she was when she didn't have to hunch over to compensate for her partner's lack of height. She was also keenly aware that she was babbling, something she tended to do when she was ill at ease.

As if on cue, the musicians started a new song. "Very well," Colin said, grasping her hand and escorting her onto the ballroom floor. "Let's dance."

They both automatically assumed proper posture and positioning. Then Colin led her around the floor.

"I do not understand," Lily said after a few moments of some rather enjoyable dancing. He filled her expectations nicely. "Why are you asking me to dance? I am a common criminal, after all."

Colin looked directly at her, their noses practically touching. "I promise not to bring up that unpleasantness if you do not, my lady."

Her brows lifted. She could see he was serious. He wasn't interested in rubbing his supposed suspicions in her face. Instead, he seemed to concentrate his energies on the dance. Relief flowed through her at not having to fend off his allegations, and she followed suit, determined to take pleasure in the moment.

Lily had certainly told the truth regarding her skill, Colin thought. She was an excellent dancer and light on her feet. She seemed to effortlessly follow his lead, and her anticipation of his turn of direction was flawless. On top of that, he considered it his good fortune that she didn't feel compelled to fill the silent void between them with empty-headed prattle, or worse, an argument. The last thing he wanted—or needed—was a scene. In his experience the young ladies of the *ton* thrived on drama, especially if they were at the center of it. Thus her silence suited him fine. At least for the first minute of the dance.

Then, unbelievably, *he* began to experience an urge

to engage her in conversation. It felt more than a little odd to be dancing with someone who was mute. Especially when she hadn't given him a direct look since they had stepped onto the dance floor.

She had looked up, down, and all around, which had been awkward, to say the least, in light of their similarity in height. Not that he minded her being so tall. It was rather refreshing not to have to keep looking down at his dance partner. However, it was blatantly obvious that she was doing her best to pay attention to everyone and everything *except* him, which was something he was unaccustomed to, particularly in the company of a young lady firmly entrenched in the marriage mart.

"Lady Lily," he began, concentrating as he always did when he said her name so as not to verbally trip over it. "Do you find my countenance so offensive that you are unable to look at me?"

She blinked. Now he had her attention. Her gaze met his, her dark eyes as wide and round as china saucers. Yet she recovered from her shock quickly. "Lord Chesreton, surely by the admirable glances of all the ladies here you are more than aware that your countenance is beyond superb. I am also sure that this isn't the first time you have been complimented thusly."

Well. What did one say to that bit of buttering up? He searched her face, fully expecting to find a lack of sincerity there. But Lady Lily apparently said precisely what she meant, for her expression was genuine.

And expectant. Colin realized she was waiting for him to compliment her likewise. It would be, after all, the polite thing to do when one received a few words of obsequiousness. He'd liked to have told her she was a diamond of the first water, if only in response to her totally candid remark to him.

Except that he couldn't.

She wasn't pretty, at least not by current society's standards. Her black hair was arranged in some kind of intricate coil of braids and limp curls, but the hairstyle did nothing to accentuate her face. Instead it seemed to exhibit her in an unflattering way. Her features were unremarkable, although he did notice she possessed a long, slender neck. However, he couldn't possibly compliment her neck, not without coming across like a complete imbecile.

He did decide that her gown was indeed lovely, comprised of some kind of white silky material decorated with what seemed like hundreds of twinkling clear stones. Even he could appreciate the effort it must have taken to hand stitch each one in place. They sparkled and shimmered beneath the chandelier lights, as if she were covered with tiny stars. He was confident that any kind word said about it would be well received, even if the dress hung on so thin a frame that a slight London breeze might send her flying like a kite into the air. Possessing two sisters gave him insight to the importance of fashion to women.

"My lady, if I may say—"

"Yes?" she interjected, this time looking directly at him. Her face was so honestly open he suddenly felt under extreme pressure to say exactly the right thing.

"Your gown is beautiful," he began. "You have prime taste in clothing."

From her fallen expression, he had said exactly the *wrong* thing.

"Thank you," she mumbled. "I will be sure to tell Mother." She averted her eyes again, succeeding in making him feel like a heel.

But he didn't try to decipher her cryptic comment. Women were often saying and doing things he didn't understand, something he learned growing up with three of the fairer sex. Many times it was easier to let things be. It certainly alleviated a lot of potential headaches.

They had just completed a turn on the floor when she suddenly yelped in apparent pain.

Colin stopped and immediately saw the origin of her distress.

A large glob of melted wax had landed on her shoulder, near her exposed collarbone. The golden mound oozed for a split-second before cooling enough to halt mid-drip. Glancing up, he saw that they were directly under the largest chandelier. Two more candles were about to spill their wax.

"Allow me." He dropped her left hand and quickly guided her to the edge of the ballroom before she was dripped on again. Without thinking he whisked off his glove and peeled away the wax from her skin, which had already started to harden. It was only when he heard her gasp that he realized he'd overstepped his bounds.

"My apologies, Lady Lily. I shouldn't have been so forward."

She fixed her eyes on the angry red mark the wax had left behind. He thought she might lash out at his boldness. But instead she simply said, "Thank you, my lord."

He had to admire her stoutness, for he could tell by the color of the welt that she had to be in pain. Yet she gave no sign of the extent of her discomfort, and she had blessedly not dissolved into a wailing pool of tears at his feet.

Knowing it would be boorish of him not to attend to her further, he grasped her hand and said, "Come with me."

Chapter Seven

"Where are we going?" Lily asked, following at Colin's heels.

"To the terrace."

Lily goggled at her gloved hand enfolded in his bare one. She could hardly suppress the shiver at the memory of his fingers brushing against her collarbone as he removed the warm candle wax. She tried to shove the thought—and the tingle—away. But it wasn't working. Not when the burning pain she was experiencing reminded her of the feather-light feeling of his palm touching her skin.

The large balcony, thank goodness, was empty. Like the rest of the house, it had been decorated with what seemed like hundreds of flickering tapers.

She would never look at a candle the same way again.

She followed him into a fairly secluded corner, where

water bubbled and flowed in a marble fountain decorated with sculpted turtle doves. He released her hand and retrieved a white handkerchief from the inside pocket of his dress coat, then dipped it into the running water. Before she understood his intentions, he pressed the cool, wet cloth to her shoulder, soothing the burn.

"May I?" he asked belatedly.

Speech abandoned her at that point. So did rational thought and the act of breathing. She surmised that this entire scene was highly improper, and that her chaperone, who tonight was her usually occupied mother, would have swooned at the sight of Baron Chesreton dabbing at her daughter's bare skin with his handkerchief. Not to mention that up to this point she had staunchly sworn off men and branded them all boors.

But truly, propriety and all that rot didn't matter one little bit to Lily right now, not while she was enjoying Colin's ministrations far too much.

He stopped dabbing. "Has the pain lessened?"

"Yes." Actually, she wasn't feeling any pain at all. He was so close to her she could smell the clean scent of his aftershave and sense the warmth radiating from him. It encircled her like a comforting cloud.

"Good." Colin removed his handkerchief and stuck it in the water again, then squeezed out the excess. This time he handed it to her. "Keep it," he said. "You may have need of it later."

He was perhaps the most considerate man she had ever met. And the most confusing. He thought her a thief, yet he asked her to dance, and then took care of her wound as if they were the closest of acquaintances. Her thoughts were nearly as jumbled as her emotions.

Suddenly she heard a rustling sound, followed by a mumbled oath. She gawked at Colin. "Did you hear that?"

He pressed his finger to her lips and nodded. Together they crouched behind the fountain in time to see someone dressed in dark clothing descending the trellis outside the Balcarris estate.

"That's the countess' room," Colin whispered.

Excitement pulsed through Lily, so much so she barely contemplated that Colin was touching her again. On the lips this time. She would dissect that interesting bit of contact at a later time, but right now her focus was on the intruder. "It is him!" she whispered against Colin's finger. "It is the burglar, I just know it!"

Colin withdrew his hand and moved away from her without uttering a sound.

Lily picked up the folds of her dress and followed him. "Where are you going?"

"To catch a thief." Colin made his way down the massive staircase, taking the steps two at a time with catlike grace.

"Not without me you do not." She hurried behind, quickly aligning herself alongside him until their steps were synchronized.

"Lily!" he hissed, casting aside formality. "Go back to the party. You have no business out here."

"And you do?"

"I am a man," he said as they both reached the bottom step at the same time.

"Thank you for informing me. I never would have figured that out for myself."

He whirled around and faced her. "You know what I mean. The cur may be armed. He could be dangerous." Colin planted his hands on her shoulders and leaned close. "This is not something a lady should be involved in."

"And while we're out here debating the sexes you are letting him get away!" Shaking off his grip, she stormed past him in the direction the thief had escaped, following the trail of broken branches in the garden shrubs.

"What did I do to deserve this?" he muttered, catching up to her.

"I heard that."

"Good."

They ventured farther into a darker part of the garden. Her foot struck something hard and solid, causing her to halt. Colin shoved into her from behind, knocking her off balance. He grabbed her arm to steady her.

"Ouch!" she cried, turning around and tossing him a glare. "Watch where you are going."

"Me?" Colin sounded like a man teetering on his last thread of patience. "You are the one who stopped dead in your tracks. Warn a mate next time, if you please."

"Um, I do say, what is this?"

Lily's head jerked around at the familiar voice. Standing in front of her, his quizzing glass held just so, one perfectly groomed eyebrow arched at an exact angle, was Michael Balcarris. He gave them a haughty look.

"What are you two doing out here in my garden?"

"Well, we were, um, you see, we—"

Colin listened as Lily did a perfectly horrid job of answering a simple question. He waited a brief moment to see if she could formulate a complete sentence. When he realized she couldn't, he intervened before her tongue had tied itself into a knot.

"Michael, old fellow!" he said, stepping forward and holding out his hand. "I have not had the opportunity to congratulate you on such a smashing ball. Well done, I must say."

"But of course." He regarded Colin with a curious eye, then Lily, then Colin again. "However, your compliment doesn't explain your presence with Lady Lily. Out here. At night. Alone." He peered around Colin's shoulder, then gave the garden a quick survey. "With no chaperone in sight."

Colin glanced at Lily. Now he did know what her guilty expression looked like, because it was as if the word were stamped all over her face. Even in the dim light of the faraway outdoor torches he could perceive her flushed cheeks and her wide-eyed stare. She also seemed to be rendered mute.

"It is all very easy to explain, Michael," Colin began, eager to rectify whatever misconstrued thoughts his former friend had bouncing around inside his head. "Lady Lily and I were on the terrace—"

"Candle wax had dripped on my shoulder," she interjected, finally finding her voice.

"And I was tending to her wound. With her permission, of course," he added quickly.

"Of course." Michael's expression remained impassive.

"As I dabbed her shoulder, we heard a noise—"

"And saw a man descending your mother's trellis!" Lily stepped in front of Colin. "It is the Bracelet Bandit, my lord, it must be. We were trying to apprehend the scoundrel."

Michael let out a haughty laugh. "You?" he said, pointing his quizzing glass at Lily. "And you?" He looked at Colin. "I daresay I've never met two more, ah, unlikely sleuths in my entire life."

"I beg your pardon?" Lily sounded deeply offended. Colin would have been offended himself, if Michael's ridiculous airs didn't have him wondering whether he should burst out laughing or strangle the irritating man. Dealing with Lord Hathery in his current persona was often terribly excruciating.

He vowed to corner him one day and find out what he was on about. Having known Michael nearly all his life, Colin was totally at sea as to what ill wind could be responsible for the earl's horrid shift in personality, as Michael had been such an easygoing individual when they were growing up. Perhaps he had fallen off his horse during his final year at Oxford. Colin had heard about people who behaved the complete opposite to their normal selves after suffering a head injury. One could only speculate in Hathery's case, of course.

"No offense intended, Lady Lily," Michael said, offering a stiff bow. "But I sincerely doubt there is anyone untoward on the premises. I have taken precautions against that, considering the misfortune that seems to have befallen our privileged society."

Colin had to force himself not to roll his eyes at Michael's haughtiness. He also needed to back up Lily's assertion, because at that moment she appeared to be twisting in the wind. "Michael, we both saw and heard the man. He shot down the trellis and ran through the garden."

"The broken branches prove it," Lily added.

Michael sniffed. "Oh, those. Mother and Tragenthorpe—he's our new butler, by the way— accidentally took a tumble the other day when they were pruning the roses. Mother's balance isn't the best these days. I fear she took the poor man right down with her."

Colin could just imagine the rather portly Countess Hathery clutching Tragenthorpe's lapels for dear life as they both went tumbling into the bushes. The man deserved hazard pay for coming through such an experience in tact.

"Be that as it may," Lily said, her hands firmly planted on her slender hips, "there was an intruder in your home. I would think you'd at least call for an inquiry of some sort."

Michael dismissed her with a limp wave. "My lady, the shadows frequently play tricks out here at night. And as for what you heard . . . well, that was just me getting some night air. It is most stuffy in the ballroom, considering the tremendous crush of people in there. Now," he said, moving toward Lily and Colin and making a shooing gesture with his hands, "both of you must return to the party at once, before you are missed. You know how idle tongues love to wag at these, ah, events. People might take your absence as something more than it really is."

"But my lord—"

"Lily." Colin laid his hand on her arm. It was obvious Michael didn't believe them. Why should he? They had no solid proof that anyone had actually been upstairs in the house. Not to mention that now he wondered if his mind had been playing tricks on him too. "Michael is right. We should return."

She opened her mouth as if to say something, then clamped it shut. "Fine," she said through tight lips. "We'll go inside."

"Splendid!" Michael called after them. "And do visit the dessert table while you are there. The aspic is to die for."

"Will do," Colin said, escorting Lily back up the stairs. He could practically see the steam spouting from her ears. But there was nothing they could do, at least not at the moment.

"Colin," Lily said, stopping before they exited the balcony and entered the ballroom. "Do you think Michael is acting strangely?"

"Michael is always acting strangely."

"No, he's behaving more oddly than usual." She turned to him, lowering her voice. "If someone told you they saw a trespasser climbing out of your mother's window, would you brush them off like a pesky fly?"

"No." He turned around and looked down the staircase. Michael was near the bottom, picking at his fingernails, as if he hadn't a care in the world.

"Colin."

He looked at Lily. For the first time doubt had seeped into her eyes—more than likely the same doubt he'd experienced moments ago. But what were the chances both of them saw something that was actually nothing?

"You did see someone escape down the trellis, didn't you?"

"Yes," he said, extending his arm to her. After she linked her hand through the crook he gave it a reassuring pat. "I saw the same thing you did."

She expelled a deep breath. "I suppose you now believe that I am not a thief?"

He looked at her. "I never truly thought so, Lily."

She smiled, peering at him from beneath lowered lashes. "What should we do now?" she asked softly.

"I do not know," he said, taking a step forward. They crossed the threshold of the ballroom. "I truly do not know."

Chapter Eight

"Lily? Lily, are you listening to me?"

Lily blinked, shaking her head as if to clear it. Emily's face came back into focus, a small frown tugging at the corners of her mouth.

"I do not believe you've heard a word I've said," Emily said, pouting.

"Of course I have," Lily fibbed, trying to remember the topic of conversation. Failing that, she looked down at the square of linen embroidery in her lap. She had managed to form all of three stitches in the entire hour since Emily had arrived for early tea at Stratsford Hall. She had only brought the needlework out to have something to do with her hands. Otherwise she feared she might shred the fabric of her dress. Her nerves were strung as tight as a violin's strings.

She glanced at the uneaten cucumber sandwiches

and the barely touched raisin scones on the glossy table in the sitting room. It seemed neither woman had much of an appetite. Jabbing her needle in the delicate cloth, she avoided her friend's questioning gaze. "You were telling me about, um . . ."

"I was telling you about someone I met at the Balcarris' last night."

"Right. Lord Hathery's party." Lily paused in mid-stitch, her needle halfway through the cloth as the events from the night before poured into her mind. For the thousandth time she replayed her and Colin's conversation with Michael. To her consternation she also replayed the dance, her skin still tingling at the memory of his fingers brushing her collarbone, her mind still reeling from his nearness. His thoughtfulness had not only surprised her, it had unnerved her as well. "Ouch!" she cried as the sharp point of the needle sank into the fleshy pad of her finger.

"Lily?"

"Sorry." She brought her bleeding finger to her mouth.

"Oh, bother," Emily muttered, tossing her unfinished embroidery on the small mahogany table next to her chair. She rose from her seat. "There you go again, off in your own little world. My goodness, one would think *you* had fallen in love with London's most exquisite man."

Emily's statement snapped Lily to attention. "Most exquisite man? Emily, what are you talking about?"

Emily closed her eyes and clasped her delicate hands

together, drawing in a dramatic breath. "I am in *love,*" she said dreamily.

"In love?" Lily repeated, stunned. This was a most unexpected revelation, one that nearly knocked her off her chair. "So quickly? And with whom?"

Emily's eyes fluttered open. They were filled with annoyance. "I've only been talking about him for the past hour."

Lily searched her mind for a moment. Then her eyes widened. "Lord Tamesbury?"

Falling back in her chair with a satisfied sigh, Emily murmured, "Gavin."

"But I thought you had only met him last evening."

"I did." Emily sighed. "How can I expect you to understand, when I hardly understand it myself?"

Lily's heart went out to her friend. "I might understand more than you think." Setting her neglected needlework aside and forcing her own issues out of her mind, she took one of Emily's hands in hers. "Tell me about him."

A look of sheer delight crossed Emily's face. "Oh, Lily, he's so handsome. His eyes are a most prime shade of dark green, with little flecks of gold in them. Did you know that?"

Lily shook her head.

"And he's utterly charming, for there was never a lull in conversation during our dance. He's the very best dancer, not once did he glance at his feet while we were on the ballroom floor. He's simply . . . simply . . ."

"Perfect?"

Emily's eyes lit up. "Exactly."

Lily released Emily's hand and rose from her chair. Crossing the room, she went to the large window that overlooked the lush rose garden, now in full bloom. A warm summer breeze carried the scent of the blossoms through the slight opening in the window sash, their aroma overpowering the usually unpleasant city smell of London in June.

Although Lily had once been engaged, she didn't know what it was like to truly be in love. She had thought she had loved George, but that entire relationship had been based on lies. "How does one know when it is love?" she asked aloud, more to herself than to Emily.

She heard the rustle of Emily's skirts from behind, and soon her friend joined her at the window.

"My heart twists when I think of Gavin," Emily whispered. "I close my eyes and picture his glorious face, remember the strength of his arms around me as we danced . . . and I cannot breathe. I am in sweet agony until I see him again." She turned to Lily, her features solemn except for the tiny sparkle in her blue eyes. "If that isn't love, what is?"

Lily inhaled a sharp breath as once again she visualized her dance with Colin. Love and Colin—those were two words had no business being in the same sentence, since she could barely abide the man. Turning, she forced her focus back on Emily. "Is it wise to entertain such ideas? Especially when you know next to nothing about Lord Tamesbury?"

With a shrug, Emily returned her attention to the window. "Why not? I've met many eligible gentlemen since my debut, and none of them can hold a candle to Gavin. He's perfect in every way." She grinned slyly. "Besides, my intention is to find out *everything* about him."

Lily couldn't help but chuckle at Emily's unabashed determination. "Within the bounds of propriety, I hope?"

Emily's bright laugh filtered through the room. "Naturally. I would not do anything to embarrass Mama. She would have a fit if I did, and I would never hear the end of it."

A wave of guilt briefly washed over Lily. Emily was being so candid with her, baring her heart basically, and Lily couldn't return the favor and tell her about the current conundrum she and Colin were in. She couldn't discuss it with anyone, except Colin himself, and she was dying to talk to him.

Emily checked the gold watch fob pinned to her lapel. "Botheration, I must be off. I have an appointment with mother and Diana. It seems I get to spend the rest of the afternoon listening to the modiste prattle on and on about how perfect Diana's figure is. Then she'll get to me." Emily held her hands together and lifted her chin, peering down her nose in an imitation of the dressmaker. " 'Tut, tut, Miss Emily. I believe we'll have to let your dress out another inch or so. Perhaps you should have a few less biscuits at dinner time.' "

Lily frowned. "You are exaggerating."

"Hardly." She placed her hands on the sides of her hips. "I fear they are expanding daily. Mama tried to make me feel better by assuring me I will have an easy time bearing children, but it doesn't help." Before Lily could comment Emily reached for her wrap. "Oh, I almost forgot. Mama told me right before I left that Lady Hathery was robbed last night."

Lily froze, staring at Emily in disbelief. "How could you possibly forget something like that?"

Emily grinned sheepishly. "My mind has been otherwise occupied, as you now know." She reached up and kissed Lily's cheek. "I shall see you soon?"

"Yes," Lily said, returning the kiss rather absently. Already her mind was whirring. Emily, her mother, and her sister would be gone from home for the rest of the day. Leaving Colin on his own. If he was home, that is. Hopefully he was. She had also been wracking her mind for an excuse to talk to him about last night. Now she had one.

Gavin Tamesbury gave Colin a broad smile. "I've met the most exquisite woman, Colin."

"Bully for you." Colin continued to stare out the window, still thinking about Lily and the Bracelet Bandit. They were pretty much the only things he was capable of thinking about.

"She's a diamond of the first water," Gavin continued, as if Colin had commented with gusto. "Her beauty lights up the room when she walks in. Her skin is as white as alabaster, her eyes like two sparkling sapphire jewels . . . her ears as big as silver platters."

Colin turned around. "Her ears?"

"Ah, so you were listening . . . sort of."

"Sorry." He walked over to the chair by the hearth and sat down across from his friend. The man had arrived a few moments ago, insistent on seeing him. But Colin was finding it more difficult by the moment to concentrate on Gavin's line of conversation. "You were saying?"

"I was saying that I have met the woman of my dreams."

"That's marvelous, Gavin, but certainly you could have told me this at a later time." *Like after I've figured out what to do about Lily.*

"You do not understand." Gavin leaned forward. "The exceptional creature I am talking about is your sister."

Colin blinked. Twice. "My sister?" His mind wandered to the Hathery's party last night, and he remembered Gavin's dance with Emily. He shook his head and gave Gavin a warning look. "She's too young for you," he stated firmly.

Gavin furrowed his brows. "But she's two and twenty."

"Emily is seventeen," Colin corrected.

"Not Emily," Gavin said quickly. "Oh, do not get me wrong, she's a lovely young girl, very sweet." An impassioned expression crossed his features. "But the woman I am referring to is Diana."

"Diana?" Colin scratched his head, befuddled. "But Gavin, you've met her on several occasions. You never spoke about her this way before."

Gavin sprung from his chair and began to pace, nervous energy radiating from him. "Yes, I realize that. I also know you must think I am daft for acting this way, but I cannot help it. Last night, when she was out on the dance floor, gliding around like an angel, it was as if I'd never seen her before." He held out his hands, palms up. "As preposterous as it sounds, I believe I have fallen in love with her."

Colin remained very still. "You've what?"

"I know, I know." Gavin resumed pacing. "Believe me, I find this to be most unexpected myself."

"To say the least."

"But I cannot help it. I truly believe she is the woman God has set apart for me."

"You've really gone round the bend, you know that Gav? How can you possibly be sure that you and my sister are divinely ordained to be together?"

"I just . . . know." Gavin stopped pacing and sat down on the chair across from Colin. "I know this might sound silly, but I've been praying for a wife."

Colin arched a brow. "It doesn't sound silly. Surprising, but not silly."

"My parents had a less than stellar marriage, as you—and most of the *ton,* unfortunately—are well aware of."

Colin nodded, growing serious. The Parringers' ill-fated marriage was the stuff of legend. Some of their public rows were still being gossiped about ten years after Gavin's father's death. Colin was surprised his friend wasn't soured on matrimony completely.

"I'd like to ask your permission to call on her."

"Wait just a minute." Colin held up his hand. He needed more than a few minutes to process the idea of Diana and Gavin. Not that he would mind Gavin as a prospective brother-in-law. But his friend was known to wear his heart on his sleeve—and it would not take Diana more than a moment to crush it into pieces, if she did not return his affections. Which he was fairly certain she didn't. "Really, Gav, I am not in the position to make these decisions."

"You most certainly are." Gavin seemed confused. "As the baron, and in your deceased father's stead, you are in a prime position to approve your sisters' suitors."

"That's not what I meant. I cannot speak for Diana, I never could. She has always chosen her own suitors."

"For goodness sake, Ches, I am not asking you to post the banns yet. I merely want permission to pay her a call."

Colin hesitated. "All right," he finally agreed. "But I must warn you that my sister can be rather . . . headstrong, to put it mildly."

"I like a woman who presents a challenge."

"Good luck, then," Colin said. "I suspect you are going to need it."

After Gavin left in an even better mood than when he had arrived, Colin returned to his room. He stripped off his jacket and waistcoat and again thought about last night. Obviously Lily wasn't the thief, and he felt remorse at believing even for a moment that she was.

Which left the disturbing knowledge that the burglar was still out there, perhaps planning his next move.

He lay back on the bed and closed his eyes, his hands clasped behind his head. But instead of the shadowy figure of a man skittering down a trellis, Lily's face swam before him. Their dance. The charming way she lost her composure when confronted by Michael. A sudden jolt ran through him.

His eyes flew open. Why was he thinking about her in such pleasant terms? Lily was a headstrong, stubborn, confounding woman. He had no doubt she would drive any man crazy. She had started sending him round the bend already.

He closed his eyes again, pushing all thoughts and images of Lily out of his mind and forcing his body to relax. He had to figure out what to do next. He was completely nonplussed at being involved in this mess. Should he go to the Bow Street Runners and tell them what he knew? He quickly nixed the idea. He knew very little, and he would probably be greeted with the same skepticism Michael had displayed. Colin frowned. *What to do, what to do . . .*

"My lady, this is highly improper," Hannah said, picking up her skirt and chasing after Lily, who was headed down the stone steps outside Stratsford Hall to the carriage awaiting them in the street. The two women were on their way to the Dymoke residence. "Not to mention a really bad idea."

"You were all for it when I said you might have a

chance to see Trevor." Lily accepted the driver's hand as he extended it to her.

"But upon further examination," Hannah quickly followed her mistress inside, "and having come to my senses . . . what I'm trying to say, my lady, is that nothing good can come of this."

Lily adjusted her dress as she sat back in the seat. "You have nothing to worry about. Mother and Father trust you implicitly. They trust me implicitly. You and I have been to the Dymokes' before. We have done nothing to arouse their suspicions."

"But my lady—"

Lily reached for Hannah's hand. "I promise, if anything happens, I will bear full responsibility. I will admit to coercing you to accompany me."

"Which you did."

"Yet it did not take much effort on my part, not with Trevor as an incentive."

Hannah's cheeks flushed, but she didn't respond.

Lily chose not to press the issue further. Hannah would reveal her thoughts and feelings about Trevor when the time was right. At the moment Lily needed to steady her own nerves. While she spoke with confidence to Hannah, inside she was a quivering mess. If she were to be caught . . . but she dismissed that possibility completely. She had to talk to Colin about what they had seen in the Balcarris garden last night. And with a little help from Hannah, she would be able to do just that.

* * *

"My lady, Miss Dymoke isn't here at the moment," Blevins said crisply.

"She isn't?" Lily breezed past the butler and entered the foyer, all the while praying for forgiveness for the little lies about to spill from her lips. Hannah followed behind her, just before the butler shut the door. "Emily said she would be here. I needed to borrow a book from her."

"Perhaps you can come back another time." Blevins crossed in front of her, blocking her from further entering the residence. "When Miss Dymoke is present."

"Then is Lord Chesreton in? I am sure he can get the book for me."

"My lord is in his suite, my lady. He has asked not to be disturbed. Again, if you can come back another time, that would be best."

Lily looked at the stern-faced man and quickly reformulated her plan. Steeling herself, she said, "I am afraid that won't be possible. See, I simply must have this book today. It is of the uppermost importance."

"Really." The butler peered at her with dubious eyes.

"I also know exactly where it is. In her bedroom." She moved closer to the butler and tried to pour on the charm. Which was difficult, since she never really possessed much charm. "Please. You would do me a tremendous favor. And I am sure Emily would not mind—we are best friends you know."

Blevins looked at Hannah. "Perhaps I can send your maid to fetch it."

"No!" both women exclaimed at once. Lily glanced at her maid, whose complexion appeared very pale. For once Lily could read her expression, and it wasn't a pleasant one. Remorse traveled through her as she realized what she was asking of the young woman. She could easily be put out by her parents for Lily's subterfuge. Not to mention what her parents would do to her. Now she was beginning to realize what an ill-conceived idea this was. But she had to press on; she hadn't come this far to turn tail and run.

"Hannah doesn't know where the book is," Lily explained, relieved that her voice sounded calm. "I would very much like for her to accompany me as I go get it. We will only be a moment."

Blevins' expression softened as he considered her request. "Very well," he said, stepping aside. "As long as you are certain Miss Dymoke won't be upset—"

"Oh, no, no," Lily said, hurrying toward the staircase before the man changed his mind. She rushed Hannah along. "She's such a generous girl."

"That she is, my lady."

"We will only be a moment." With hastened steps they ascended the staircase, and slipped inside Emily's room and closed the door. She looked at the other oak door on the opposite side of the room.

The door that separated Emily's bedroom from Colin's.

"Wait here," she instructed Hannah. "If you hear someone coming, knock three times."

"My lady," Hannah gasped, as she realized what Lily planned to do. "You cannot seriously be considering going into Lord Chesreton's private chambers."

"Only to wake him. I have to talk to him, Hannah."

"My lady, I will not allow it!"

Lily looked at her maid. The young woman held such a resolute expression, one Lily had never seen before. She was also right. Fortunately at least one of them hadn't taken leave of their senses. "Very well. I will merely knock on the door and ask for an audience."

Hannah's expression softened slightly. "That would be much more appropriate, my lady. Although I suppose there is no way I could talk you out of this completely?" As Lily shook her head, Hannah said, "I didn't think so."

Relieved that her maid finally acquiesced, Lily strode over to the door and knocked.

Chapter Nine

Colin felt a tickle on his nose, accompanied by a loud purring sound. "Get away," he mumbled, brushing off the cat but not opening his eyes. Emily's pet, Bronwyn, had the annoying habit of waking a person up, whether in the morning or during a nap—something he was in the middle of at the moment. Just as he rolled over on his side he heard a knock at the door.

"Colin?"

His eyes flew open at the sound of Lily's voice coming from the other side of the door. Pausing, he waited to see if he was hearing things.

"Colin! It's me, Lily!"

Her voice was a half whisper, half yell. What the devil did she want? Bolting out of bed, he thrust open the door. "What are you doing here?" he asked, his tone tinged with grumpiness. He never had liked being awakened out of a sound sleep.

"We need to talk."

"Now?"

"Yes, now."

He ran his hand through his hair. He'd never met such a persistent individual. "How did you manage to get by Blevins?"

"It took some . . . persuading."

Colin hardly thought his butler would allow Lily to come upstairs unescorted. Then he heard the rustling of fabric as Lily's maid made her presence known. At least she had an escort. "Wait a few moments. I'll meet you downstairs."

Lily turned to her maid and whispered. The young woman stepped away, still within sight but out of earshot. "I thought we could talk out here," Lily whispered. "More privacy."

"Lily, this is highly improper—"

"Colin, this isn't some silly ploy. Lady Hathery was robbed last night."

"I am well aware of that."

Her brows lifted with surprise. "You are? And you didn't pay me a call?"

Fisting his hands together, Colin strove for patience. "Lily, you have to go. Now."

"But—"

"I will speak with you about this downstairs. Meet me in the library. No, on second thought, in the drawing room. And keep the door *open*. Wide open." He reached out and placed his hand on the back of her waist, gently pushing her forward. "I'll see you in a few minutes."

"You promise?"

He let out an exasperated sigh. This woman would be the death of him, he just knew it. "I promise."

Lily paced back and forth across the multi-patterned Ausbusson carpet in the Dymoke drawing room. What had she been thinking, sneaking up to Colin's room? She didn't care one whit about her reputation, but she would die before she would embarrass her parents. And how unfair of her to even put Colin in such a position.

She owed him an apology. A very large one. She also owed Hannah one and intended to give her one when they returned home. At the moment her maid was sitting in the corner of the room, trying to appear inconspicuous, all the while looking as if she'd rather be anywhere than at the Dymoke residence.

Continuing to pace, Lily threaded her fingers together, and glanced toward the open door. Blevins had already passed by it—twice—giving her suspicious glances each time. Lily thought the man understood exactly what was going on, but to her great fortune had decided not to make an issue of it. And even though she finally realized she had narrowly escaped a disaster of her own doing, she still couldn't keep the image of a slumberous Colin out of her head.

When he had appeared at the door, her breath had caught. He looked so boyishly disheveled. Warmth had traveled through her, a sensation she had never felt before, not even with George.

She halted her steps. Why did she keep thinking about him this way, especially when there were more important things to focus on? *I certainly don't need this right now . . .*

"Need what?"

Lily spun around, not realizing she had spoken aloud. For the second time that hour her breathing betrayed her. He had freshened up. His hair was neatly combed, and he was wearing a smart paisley-patterned waistcoat and jacket. Unkempt or well groomed, Colin Dymoke was an exquisite-looking man.

He moved toward her. "You were saying?"

She spun away from him, feeling heat suffuse her cheeks. "Nothing, really. Just voicing my thoughts out loud."

"Very well then." He walked around her and gestured to a chair in front of the hearth. "Please, sit down." He lowered himself into the chair opposite her. "Now we can talk. You were telling me about Lady Hathery . . ."

"Yes, that's right." Relieved to get to the matter at hand, she leaned forward. "We have to go back to Michael Balcarris'."

Colin shook his head. "Absolutely not."

Lily blinked. That wasn't the answer she had expected. "Of course we do! We have to look for clues, find proof of the burglar's—"

"First of all, I am sure Michael has already had his premises thoroughly inspected. Second of all, what did you plan to do, sneak into the countess' bedroom like you did mine?"

"I didn't sneak. I knocked." She looked at her lap. "And . . ."

"Yes?"

She glanced up, and caught the corner of his lips twitch. The bounder, he was enjoying her discomfiture. "I believe I owe you somewhat of an apology."

He arched his brow in an exaggerated way, not unlike Michael. "Somewhat? You barge into my room—"

"I did *not* barge, and I never entered your room—"

"Waking me up from the most delightful of naps, whereas I was the king of England, surrounded by servants there to do my every bidding . . ."

"Now you are just teasing." Lily tried to suppress a smile, but failed.

"True, I am teasing." He grinned, but soon it faded. "However, I am not teasing about this. We are not going to Michael's to hunt for clues or search his house or do anything of the sort. Leave that to the authorities."

"But—"

"Hold on." He held up his hand. "I agree we cannot sit around and do nothing."

"Thank you," she said, relieved they were both finally in accord with something.

"So I will visit a few of the gentlemen clubs and discern what I can. I am sure there's bound to be some talk about last night." He rose from his chair, gesturing for her to follow suit. Then he crossed the room and went to the open doorway. "I will send word to you when I find out something. Now, did you bring a coach or shall I have my driver take you home?"

Dismissed. She sucked her breath through her teeth. Not a very ladylike gesture, but she was hardly feeling ladylike at the moment. "Colin, you will not treat me like a child."

"I wasn't aware I was."

"Sending me home to sit on my hands while you are out having fun hardly puts us on equal footing."

"Fun?" He moved closer to her. "Lily, criminal conduct is not fun. Chasing down a criminal when you have no experience and no authority is not fun. It is dangerous, reckless . . ."

"And most exciting . . . do you not agree?"

Colin marveled at Lily. Her eyes were sparking with fervor, her complexion rosy with anticipation. She truly did think all this was exciting. And if he admitted the truth to himself, he had to agree. The thought of finding out information, of discovering something that might apprehend the thief, made his blood run a little faster too. He was surprised to realize he and Lily were kindred spirits in that respect.

Still, they were both amateurs. And she was a lady. The daughter of a duke. He couldn't allow her to put herself in harm's way, which she would undoubtedly do once given the chance. He had never met anyone more impulsive or reckless, man or woman. No, he had no other choice but to convince her to go home, and to wait. Even though he knew it would be difficult for her in the extreme. Still, it was for her own good.

"Lily, listen to me. Please." Before he could stop himself he was touching her shoulders. He should probably let her go, but he didn't want to. He wanted to make sure she would take him seriously. "I promise, as soon as I find out anything, I will come to you. It is the best way to go about this."

She seemed to consider his words for a moment. Then her shoulders slumped beneath his palms. "You are right, of course," she said, moving away. "I should go home. That is where I belong." Her look was sharp. "But the minute you learn something you let me know. Do not make me come after you."

His lips curved into a smile. "Do not worry, my lady. I won't."

After escorting both Lily and her maid out the front door, he watched Lily get inside the carriage, remaining on the front sidewalk until she disappeared from view toward the direction of her home. Satisfied, he went back inside, retrieved his hat, and left for White's.

Lily peeked through the carriage window, straining to see the Dymoke house. She could barely make it out, but she watched as Colin went back inside. With a smile she leaned back in her seat.

"Oh no," Hannah said.

"What do you mean, 'Oh no'?"

"We are not going home, are we? Even though Lord Chesreton specifically requested that we do."

A pinprick of guilt stabbed at her. Since this morning she had been less than forthright with her best friend, lied to a butler, dragged her maid with her and tried to sneak into an unmarried gentleman's bedroom, and deceived him into thinking she was acquiescing to his request. The prick turned into a stab. To say she had engaged in bad behavior was an understatement. But didn't the end justify the means? There was a rampant thief pilfering the *ton*. She was one of two witnesses to the perpetrator. And the other witness insisted on tying her hands behind her back, so to speak. What recourse did she have?

Lily tapped the roof of the carriage.

"Yes, my lady?" came the driver's muffled voice.

"Take me to the Balcarris estate."

"Yes, my lady."

Hannah groaned.

It didn't take long to reach Michael's house. Lily instructed James to return in one half hour. She didn't care where he went, just as long as her vehicle wasn't seen near the house. The day was turning to evening, and clouds now cloaked the sky. No one appeared to be about. She was thankful for small favors. She turned to Hannah. "Now, just—"

"I know. Just wait for you here at the gate. Shall I whistle like a lark three times if I see anyone coming? Or perhaps twitter like a robin?"

Lily frowned. "Sarcasm does not become you," she remarked.

"Sorry, my lady."

With stealthy movements she snuck into the Balcarris garden from the side gate. The strong perfume of roses and lilies filled her nostrils with their heady scent. Carefully she crept down the flagstone path, keeping her steps silent as she headed toward the terrace. Once she found the trellis, she knew she was in the right spot. Quietly she moved toward a tall, thick hedge of forsythia, near the base of the trellis. Leaning over she studied the ground for footprints. This had to be the area where the thief had landed during his escape.

Then suddenly a hand clamped over her mouth, almost taking her breath away. She felt an arm tighten around her waist, drawing her back against something hard and solid.

A scream escaped her throat as she was dragged into the hedge.

Chapter Ten

"Would you be quiet?"

Lily's eyes grew wide with shock. "Colin?" she asked. Although against his hand it sounded like "Mmph?"

"Yes. Now, if I release my hand, will you be silent?"

She nodded, and he let go.

She spun around, her skirts whirling madly around her feet. "What are you doing here?" The question practically exploded from her mouth in an indignant, but forceful whisper. "And how did you get past Hannah?"

"I grew up with Michael, remember? I know this place better than half his servants. But that is not the point. I should ask you what you are doing here. Although I won't because I already know the answer."

Her chin lifted. "I am searching for clues."

"You are defying my request," he shot back.

"Your orders, you mean." A thin branch of forsythia fell against her cheek. She brushed it back and away from her face. "If no one else will be proactive about this, then I must."

He sighed heavily. "Are you always this incorrigible?"

"Are you always this overbearing?"

"I am *not* overbearing. I've been accused of many things, but being overbearing isn't one of them."

"Oh?" By the spark in her brown eyes he could see she was intrigued. The forsythia branch tapped her face again. She batted at it. "What such things?"

"It was a figure of speech." Obviously her curiosity knew no limits, something he had suspected from the start, which was why he had backtracked and headed to Michael's house instead of White's. As he had anticipated, she was here, stirring up trouble—and now she was trying to steer him off track. "Do not change the subject. We were talking about *you* and your penchant for dishonoring your word."

Her defiant expression fell. "You left me no choice." The branch slapped against her face once more, and her brows knit together in a scowl he found rather cute. Reaching over, he snapped the offending branch with his thumb and forefinger, then tossed it aside.

"Thank you," she said, her tone and expression softening. Her eyes held a touch of meekness, an emotion he hadn't seen from her before. He'd witnessed her curiosity and most definitely her obstinacy. Yet this . . . vulnerability . . . was altogether new. It tugged at something inside him, giving him pause. He had a sudden, *genuine* urge to protect her, which surprised him, since she didn't give the appearance of needing protecting at all—except maybe from herself.

"I suppose you'll send me on my way," she said, sounding dejected. "Again."

"I probably should."

She nodded. "I guess I shouldn't expect anything different from you. After all, a stolen bracelet never ended up in your possession."

Her words struck him, hitting him hard. She was right. He didn't have as much at stake in this as she did. For once he understood her fervor. He paused for a moment, knowing he would end up regretting speaking his next words, but saying them anyway. "I suppose since we're already here . . ."

"Wonderful, Colin!" Her face lit up in a smile, one he was tempted to return. "I am glad to see you've come to your senses after all."

His partial grin disappeared, and he couldn't help feeling as if he'd been somewhat played. "My senses aren't the ones in question, my lady."

"Right, right." Her response wasn't spoken directly to him, but rather to the ground she was currently examining as if she were a seasoned detective. "I thought I saw something near here."

"Such as?"

"I am not sure. Something just seems . . . off to me."

Colin joined her search. After a few futile moments he said, "Perhaps you were mistaken. There is nothing here. Not even a footprint." Something Colin found quite odd himself, now that he thought about it.

"You give up too easily." She placed her gloved hands on her narrow waist. "There must be a clue here somewhere. No thief is perfect. I am sure if we . . ."

Her words faded in Colin's ear as he heard a faint rustle of branches. Grabbing Lily, he yanked her beside him and crouched down behind the hedge.

"I beg your—"

"Shh." With a jerk of his thumb he gestured in the direction of the noise.

Her eyes grew wide, but she remained silent. He was relieved she decided to listen to him for once.

"What ho! Who do we have here?"

Colin looked up. Peering over the hedge, through his quizzing glass, and managing to appear both bored and mildly inquisitive at the same time, was Michael Balcarris. Yet again.

"Well, isn't this interesting. Most interesting, indeed."

Michael's brow arched in his usual impertinent way, which Lily found quite irritating, even more than she usually did. She rose to a standing position, Colin following suit. Her cheeks warmed, betraying the guilty emotions coursing through her at being seen snooping in his garden. Colin had warned her, but she hadn't really thought they'd get caught. Truth be told she hadn't thought this through at all. "Th-this isn't what it looks like," she stammered.

Michael lowered his glass. "Really," he replied

drolly. "I say, I am most curious as to what exactly *this* is. Because it appears to me that you and my good friend Lord Chesreton are trespassing on my premises. And alone, once again."

"Not trespassing—" Lily began.

"I can explain—" Colin said at the same time.

They both looked at each other. Lily could see that Colin was as flustered as she was. Then an idea came to mind. Thrusting her hands behind her back, she removed one of her gloves and flung it behind her.

"Lord Hathery, I apologize. I somehow misplaced one of my gloves last eve. Lord Chesreton was kind enough to assist me in finding it."

Colin glanced in her direction, his expression puzzled. With a sharp jerk of her head she indicated to him the position of the glove. Taking her cue, he looked behind her.

"Ah!" he said, a little more stiffly than she would have liked, but still convincingly enough. "Uh, I see it now." Stepping behind her he retrieved the glove and handed it to her.

"I am forever in your debt." She looked at Michael out of the corner of her eye, gauging his reaction.

He observed all of this with his usual bored expression. "Tut, tut," he said. "If that was all, why didn't you just send your maid to look for it? I saw her just beyond the garden gate. I sent her home, by the way, in my personal carriage. She appeared most nervous; I thought perhaps she was ill. She had insisted on staying, but I really though it best to send her on. Or you could have simply asked me for assistance. I would have happily helped you find your . . . missing glove."

His knowing tone didn't sit well with her, and she wondered if he believed them at all. But the earl's expression was inscrutable. "I didn't want to bother you," she insisted, moving to walk past him. "My sincerest apologies for putting you out. I promise it won't happen again. Now that I—excuse me, *we've*—found my glove, we should take our leave. I must see to Hannah straightaway. Right Co—uh, Lord Chesreton?"

"Yes—right." Colin seemed to regain his equanimity. He also seemed to be in as much of a hurry to leave as she. Stepping forward, he started scooting past Michael. "Be seeing you soon, Hathery."

But the earl moved in front of them, stopping them in their tracks. "Just a moment. I had no idea you two were on such . . . *friendly* terms."

"We hardly know each other," Colin quickly said. "She's a friend of my sister Emily."

"Ah, yes. Emily."

Lily thought she detected a change in Michael's eyes. A softening, as if a pleasant thought or image had passed through his mind. But it swiftly disappeared, so quickly she was certain she imagined it.

"My lady must be a very good friend of Lady Emily's for you to go to all this trouble." Michael lifted his glass again and peered at Colin, then at Lily. "In fact, one would think that Emily isn't the only Dymoke to appreciate Lady Lily's . . . friendship."

Michael's implication was clear. Lily felt her cheeks

color and she couldn't help but look at Colin. Her heart flipped, then flopped at the thought of him having any interest in her beyond loyalty to his sister. Memories flooded over her as she thought about the past couple days. The kindness he exhibited, without hesitation, when the candle wax dripped on her. The tickle in her belly when he had stood so close to her on the balcony. The tiny act of consideration when he'd dispensed with the annoying forsythia branch mere moments ago.

She knew she should deny Michael's supposition. It would be the right—and truthful—thing to do. There was nothing between her and Colin other than their knowledge of the bracelet planted in her cloak. But when she tried to speak, the words would not form on her tongue. And suddenly she started rationalizing something she had never seriously considered before: Would letting Michael believe she and Colin were together be such a bad thing?

"Now see here," Colin said, not liking Michael's implication at all. The man was being insolent and overreaching in the extreme and Colin wasn't about to let him get away with it. "As I stated before, I am merely helping out a friend of Emily's."

Michael held up his hand and waved it. "Of course you are. No need to explain any further." He leaned forward as if they shared a valuable secret. "Be assured, I shall remain most discreet."

A spike of panic drove into Colin. "But—"

"No need for thanks, my good man." Michael tapped his quizzing glass on Colin's shoulder. "Your secret is safe with me. I promise not to breathe a word of what I've seen here this evening. Not even to Mother."

Colin looked to Lily for help, but she seemed to have lost leave of her senses. A dreamy, faraway look had crept into her eyes, as if she wasn't a part of the current conversation at all.

"You two seem to have an affinity for my garden," Michael continued, ignoring Colin's assertions. "While I agree it is a lovely setting, may I recommend a few other places to conduct your trysts?"

"We are not trysting!" Colin said, raising his voice.

Michael grinned and nodded. "Of course you aren't. Now, how about we all go inside and have a spot of tea? To celebrate your 'nontrysting,' so to speak?"

Colin glanced at Lily, then nudged her with his elbow. Why wasn't she saying anything? Why was she standing there as if she couldn't comprehend the English language?

"Um . . ." she finally spoke after a lengthy pause.

Too lengthy, in Colin's opinion, only adding to the awkwardness of the situation. He had to end this and end it now, especially since Michael was determined not to believe a single one of his protestations. "My thanks, Michael, but we must be on our way. I am sure Lady Lily is expected at home soon."

"Right," she said dreamily. "On our way."

"Perhaps another time, then." Michael stepped to the side, brandishing his quizzing glass in the direction of the garden exit. "You two enjoy the rest of your evening."

As Colin hurried past with Lily in tow, he thought he saw Michael wink at him. If he had been a betting man, he would have wagered the earl had thoroughly enjoyed confounding him.

Colin, however, did not. Once he and Lily reached the blessedly deserted street, he turned to her, grasping her arm and giving it a shake. "Lily. Lily!"

At last she seemed to snap out of her stupor. "What?"

"Where is your driver?" he snapped, fighting to hold his aggravation in check. "I am assuming you didn't walk here."

"Of course not. And why are you snapping at me?"

"Why didn't you set Michael straight?" When she didn't answer right away he threw up his hands in frustration. "Oh, forget it. Where is your driver?"

"I-I am not sure." She seemed to shrink back from him. "I imagine he's at the Grey Pebble Tavern a couple streets over. He often frequents there."

Snatching her wrist, he dragged her along the sidewalk in the direction of the tavern.

"Colin. *Colin.*"

At the pleading way she said his name, he stopped. Glancing down at his hand, he realized he was holding her far too tightly. He released his grip. "Sorry," he said, storming off in search of her carriage.

"Why are you so angry?" she asked, making quick work of the distance between them.

"I am not angry."

"Upset then."

"I am not upset."

"Well, you are certainly something because a cheerful person doesn't drag a woman down the street, then storm off like a spoiled child."

"Spoiled?" He halted his steps. "You are accusing me of being spoiled? I suggest you visit a looking glass sometime in the near future."

"I am not spoiled," she said, drawing an indignant breath. "I may be an only child—"

"Who is used to getting her way under all circumstances, no matter what the damage to people around her. That, my lady, is the very definition of spoiled." He spun around and walked away again.

"I hardly get my way all the time," she said, catching up to him. "And I do not think you know me well enough to make such a blanket accusation about me."

"Oh, believe me, my lady, I know enough."

"Colin, I do not see what you are so out of sorts about. Michael has no idea why we were really snooping in his garden."

"No. Instead he thinks we were trysting," he muttered, not bothering to hide his annoyance. "And you let him believe it. You just stood there with a vacuous, insipid look on your face, not saying a single word."

When he didn't sense her beside him, he slowed his

steps, then stopped completely. He turned around to see Lily behind him, a forlorn expression on her face. She was twisting the glove she had dropped on the ground in her hands.

"Is it so horrible for him to think that?" she asked, her voice so low he could hardly hear it. "Is it such an exceedingly awful thing for you to be seen with me? I know I am no great beauty and that I am too tall and so-cially awkward—"

"Lily—" he started, then stopped speaking

"Never mind." She held up her hand, her voice qua-vering. "I do not want to know the answer." Straighten-ing, she went to him. "I can find my driver from here, Lord Chesreton. Tomorrow I will go to Lord Hathery and explain everything. I assure you I won't trouble—or humiliate—you ever again."

"Lily, you can't walk the streets alone. I'll escort you."

She didn't protest, but she didn't slow her steps ei-ther. When she reached her carriage, she immediately opened the door and went inside without giving him an-other look.

He watched as the carriage pulled away. He'd hurt her, that much was clear. And perhaps for a fleeting mo-ment that had been exactly his intentions—to cause her discomfort for once, considering she had been nothing but a piercing thorn in his side practically from the mo-ment they'd met. But he had obviously gone too far. And he certainly hadn't meant to cause her undue pain.

He needed to make amends. And he needed to do it now.

Chapter Eleven

Lily balled up the glove in her hand and flung it across the carriage. It hit against the back of the seat and plopped down onto the floor. She didn't bother to pick it up, even though it was silk and quite expensive. A little dirt on a glove didn't matter one whit. Not when the ache in her heart overshadowed everything.

She barely noticed the bumps and dips in the road as James took her back to Grosvenor Square. She was fuming. And hurt. And feeling like a foolish ninny.

And it was her own fault.

Colin had every right to be put out with her. She had not only perpetrated the lie about the glove, she had allowed Michael to jump to his own incorrect conclusions, and had done nothing to rectify them. Why had she let that happen? It was all extremely out of character for her, sneaking into gentlemen's bedrooms and lying on a regular basis. What had she reaped for it all? She was no further to discovering the truth about the Bracelet Bandit than she was two days ago. And now Colin was out of sorts. It would not surprise her if he never spoke to her again.

All that rot about the end justifying the means was dead wrong. Lying only wrought more trouble. She was a prime example of that. First thing in the morning she would set everything straight with Michael.

But fixing things with Lord Hathery would not salve her wounded emotions.

She had allowed herself a few fantastical notions concerning Colin, and she had let them bound over the wall she had carefully constructed around her heart. He certainly wasn't to blame for not wanting Michael to think he had designs on her and he had made it perfectly and painfully clear to the earl that he didn't. So she really shouldn't be upset with him. That was something he didn't deserve. Instead she was irritated with herself.

She lowered her head and rubbed her forehead with her fingers and thumb. It wasn't fair. She had spent the last few months—no years, really—wishing for someone to love her. She thought she had found that person in George, but he hadn't wanted *her*, just her money and the trappings that came with it.

Since then she had had a few gentlemen callers, even two proposals, but she would have none of it. Their intentions were so transparent, the greed so evident in their eyes and in their tone of voice that she would have had to be blind and deaf not to realize what they were truly after. She didn't want to settle for that. She wanted a marriage like her parents, who adored each other. If she couldn't have love, she would have nothing.

But nothing was becoming harder and harder to live with.

There was nothing left for her to do but to put Colin out of her mind, and her heart, once and for all. It would be difficult considering her and Emily's friendship, but she would manage it. They might run into each other every once in a while, but with Colin's penchant for travel it would not happen too frequently. She would come to a point where Colin Dymoke would not have an effect on her at all. Eventually.

And as far as the Bracelet Bandit was concerned, she would seek out the perpetrator herself. She didn't need Michael's or Colin's help. Especially Colin's. He certainly would not want to assist her after this evening's debacle anyway. If she focused all her energies in ferreting out the perpetrator then she would not have to think about Colin Dymoke at all.

She had herself nearly convinced of all that when the coach lurched to a sudden stop, yanking her out of her thoughts and almost sending her flying across the interior of the vehicle. Her hands gripped the edge of the seat for support until she regained her balance. She was straightening the crooked bodice of her dress when a knock sounded on the door.

"Yes, James?"

He opened the door. "Pardon me, m'lady," he said in

his thick Scottish burr, "but Lord Chesreton requests a word with ye."

"He does?"

"Aye. An' he's refusin' to move 'til ye speak with him."

Her driver's words confused her. "Move? Where exactly is he?"

"In front of the carriage, m'lady."

Lily leaned forward and peeked out the door. They were on a small narrow side street, one that James often took as a shortcut to bypass the carriages and phaetons that often clogged the main arteries of town. Even though the streets were practically empty, James had obviously taken the alley out of habit.

It was difficult to make out Colin's form in the shadowy evening, but she could see him standing in front of the team of horses, blocking their passage.

"Shall I physically remove him, my lady?" James' thickly mustached lip curled into a devious smile.

She had no doubt that her burly driver could easily dispense with Colin, despite the fact that Colin wasn't exactly a small man himself. "That won't be necessary, James," she said, not liking his eagerness to dispatch Colin. "I will speak with him."

"As you wish." He tipped his hat and walked away. She could hear James talking, or rather arguing, with Colin. However, within moments Colin was standing in the doorway of her carriage.

Just seeing him made her folly and missteps all the more acute. Intense embarrassment infiltrated every part of her. "What do you want?" she asked, her tone short. She wasn't in the mood to maintain perfect decorum when she really didn't want to speak with him at all.

"To apologize," he said, sounding breathless.

Her gaze shot to him, and she realized he must have run more than a couple of blocks to catch up to her. He was looking directly at her with his impossibly blue, impossibly gorgeous, and impossibly sincere eyes.

"I realize I may have inadvertently hurt your feelings, and for that I am sorry." He gave her a small smile. "I was upset, but that's no reason for me to act the cub."

Lily blinked. It was the only thing she could do. His apology was unexpected, and accompanied by the most charming smile she had ever witnessed. The man was impossible, he really was. Just when she was sure he would be out of her life for good, he wiggled his way back in without much effort. She sighed. "Colin, you do not have to apologize."

"Yes, I do."

She shook her head. "I should have corrected Michael straightaway. I was wrong for not doing so. It was also wrong of me to be so ill-tempered with you."

"Lily—"

"So if anyone needs forgiveness, it is me."

"All right, but—"

"Colin, please let me finish!"

He peered at her for a moment. "How did you manage to do that?"

"Do what?"

"Sabotage my apology."

Then he grinned, and she couldn't help but smile in return. He could be terribly cute and boyish.

"You have a lovely smile," he said suddenly.

Again, he'd managed to stun her. "I do?"

He nodded.

"You are just saying that." She looked away, at a loss at how to handle the compliment.

"No, I am not." He paused, his head tilting as he considered her for a moment. "Surely you've heard that before."

"Actually, I have not."

"But you were engaged."

"To a slimy toad of a man who never paid me a single compliment that didn't have an ulterior motive behind it."

It was his turn to look stunned. "I find that difficult to believe."

She shrugged, bitterness welling within her. "I cannot really expect you to, considering the way you are."

"The way I am? Now that's a remark I've never heard before. What do you mean by that?"

"Never mind."

"No, you cannot say something like that and then not give me an explanation. That's hardly fair play, do not you think?"

She gave him a harsh look. "Life isn't fair."

"That certainly is true. But that's not an explanation."

She let out an exasperated breath. "Colin, surely you cannot be ignorant of your, your . . ."

He continued to look befuddled. She had no choice but to speak plainly, regardless of how awkward she sounded, and how awkward this conversation was with him standing outside her carriage while she remained inside. "You are incredibly handsome." There, she said it. And she could hardly look at him now without feeling mortified.

His lips quirked up in a teasing smile. "I am?" With exaggerated movements he licked his fingertip and smoothed his brows, imitating one of the many vain dandies in the *ton*. "I had no idea," he said nasally.

"Stop it, Colin. I am being serious. You are gorgeous. As are Diana and Emily. And your mother has a dignified beauty rarely found among the senior ladies of the *ton*."

Colin grew serious. "That she has. But what of it? I still do not know what you are driving at."

"Do not you see, Colin? Things are so much easier for you. Diana is never at a lack for suitors, and soon Emily will have dashing men falling at her feet. I've witnessed firsthand the many young women tripping over each other to get your attention. All of the Dymokes are respected, well liked, and sought after." She looked down at her hands. "You won't ever have to worry about being alone."

"George." He regarded her for a moment. "That knave really hurt you, didn't he?"

His gentle tone touched her deeply, enough to bring tears to her eyes. She didn't want to speak about this with him, yet something inside compelled her too. "Yes," she finally managed. "He really did. I was quite the gudgeon as far as he was concerned. I thought he loved me. He loved everything else but me. He had me completely fooled. Did you know he had the audacity to pledge his troth to me while he was courting other women?"

Reaching into his jacket pocket Colin pulled out a white linen handkerchief. "I am sorry," he said, handing it to her.

"We seem to be saying that a lot to each other." She dabbed at her eyes, soaking up a few tears with the fine linen cloth.

"That we have."

"Well, in this case, it is not necessary. It certainly isn't your fault I caught George with another woman in his arms. On my birthday, no less. My parents had thrown a lovely fete to celebrate my birthday and engagement. George disappeared soon after the announcement, and when I found him in the garden he was kissing Penelope, the Earl of Surrey's daughter. In my own house!" She wadded the folded handkerchief in her hands. "You are not to blame that I am a fool."

"You are not a fool, Lily."

She chuckled bitterly. "I surely feel like one, believing George loved me for who I was, not for my title or dowry or position in society. When we first met, I couldn't believe my good fortune. A handsome, charming man was interested in me, plain Lily. For the first few months he said and did all the right things. It was only after I had fallen for him that I realized what he was truly up to. Apparently he thought he could have my money while carrying on with other women behind my back—never mind that he wasn't even that discreet." Despite her struggle to stop them, tears coursed down her cheeks. "I am sorry. I thought I was over this . . . over him. I should be by now."

"He's the foolish one, Lily. Not you. And you are far from plain."

She gazed at him. He wasn't giving her pity, he was comforting her and doing a very fine job of it. She should have known he'd be good at this as well. "I think you really believe that."

"I do. And do not think you have the market cornered on loneliness. A person can be surrounded by people, people who claim to adore them, and still feel all alone."

"I never really thought about it that way, but I suppose you are right." For the first time she looked at Colin in a new way. Not as a handsome man of privilege who blithely glided through life without a care or worry, but as a fellow human being who appeared to be grappling with problems just as she was. With what she didn't know, but it made her feel less alone to know he wasn't as perfect as she had assumed.

James suddenly appeared behind Colin, suspicion crossing his features. "M'lady? Is everythin' all right? We've been gone longer than expected. We should be gettin' on our way."

Lily didn't immediately answer. Her gaze met Colin's. A connection had formed between them, a new and fragile bond borne out of their common struggle. She smiled. He returned it with a charming one of his own.

"M'lady?" James spoke more urgently, then looked at Colin. "You may be takin' yer leave now, m'lord," he said without the least bit of respect in his tone.

"No, James. We should take Lord Chesreton home—"

"That won't be necessary," Colin said, holding up his hand. "There's nothing more invigorating to the soul than a nice walk."

"Are you sure?"

"Abolutely." He touched the brim of his hat. "Good evening, Lady Lily."

"Good evening, Lord Chesreton."

After Colin left and the coach moved again, Lily leaned back in her seat, grappling with what just happened. Looking down at her lap, she saw his handkerchief, the initials *CD* monogrammed in elegant green letters. Her fingertips brushed over the exquisite stitches. She found herself wondering who had given him the cloth. His mother? One of his sisters? Or perhaps another woman, one of his many admirers? She found her last guess as valid as the other two.

Yet regardless of what the future held, of what would happen between her and Colin, she would treasure his compliment, and his kindness toward her. He hadn't made her feel foolish, he'd made her feel . . . cherished. He had understood her angst in a way no one else had. And even if it was only for a few fleeting moments, she would hold his words close to her heart for a very long time.

Chapter Twelve

"**A**re you sure you do not want to join me?" The Duchess of Breckenridge checked her image in the gilded looking glass hanging in the foyer and adjusted her chapeau. She stroked the ostrich plume that feathered over her cheekbone, then turned to Lily. "I would love nothing more than to spend the day shopping with my daughter."

Lily went to her mother and kissed the opposite, exposed cheek. "I am afraid I will have to decline, Mother," she said. "Another time, perhaps. You look lovely, by the way."

"Thank you, dear. So do you. I am glad you decided to wear the lavender day dress. It brings out your delicate complexion."

Lily thought the color made her look rather sallow, but she would not argue with her mother, especially when she was so looking forward to shopping. Normally she would accompany her, but Lily had unfinished business to attend to, the details of which she couldn't share with the duchess.

"I'm off, darling. I shall be back in a few hours."

"Ta, Mama." Lily watched her mother leave, then closed the door and grabbed the paper lying on the small marble-topped table nearby.

Her stomach grumbled. She hadn't had breakfast yet. As she made her way to the dining room, she planned out her day. After a light meal she would send a note of apology to Michael Balcarris, and tell him the truth about why she and Colin were in the garden last evening. The idea of admitting that she and Colin were anything but trysting lovers could have been mortifying, but after her talk with Colin she was eager to set things right. She was through lying and sneaking around. Once she got this last verbal misunderstanding taken care of she would feel much better.

Settling herself at the table, she waited for breakfast to be served. Snapping open the paper, she perused the morning headlines. Her mouth dropped open as she read the first one.

LADY LILY BRECKENRIDGE . . . A THIEF AMONG US?

"Well, this scone is as dry as dust." Diana set the crumbly pastry down on the china plate and brushed off her hands. "I believe Isabel is trying to make our meals as miserable as possible. What do you think, Colin?"

Colin stopped drumming his fingers on the breakfast room table. "Pardon?"

Diana frowned, giving him a petulant look. "I've said quite a few things, and clearly you've heard none of them. You are a million miles away. What has you so preoccupied?"

Colin picked up a raisin scone. As usual Diana had only nibbled on hers, and for once he didn't blame her. He and his sister were breaking their fast late this morn. Their mother and Emily had already left to spend the day shopping. "I am not preoccupied," he said, taking a bite of the scone. The action was against his better judgment, but at least he was occupying his mouth so he would not have to answer any more of her questions. As long as he continued chewing, anyway.

"You always were a terrible liar." She picked off a small section of another scone, frowned, then put it back.

"Hmmph." Colin had to keep from smacking his mouth in a most ungentlemanly fashion. He knew his mother kept Isabel more out of a sense of loyalty than for the woman's culinary genius. Still, it was apparent the aging cook had lost her touch. He reached for his tea and took a large gulp.

"Now that you've unsuccessfully tried to dodge my query, I am ready for your answer." Diana smiled triumphantly, and even Colin was struck by the radiance of it. His sister's beauty seemed to increase each passing day.

"I assure you I am thinking of nothing consequential. Just planning my next trip abroad." Of course that wasn't the truth, but he could hardly admit to his sister that his thoughts for the past evening and all morning had been consumed by one person—Lily. If he did he'd no doubt be barraged with questions he wasn't ready to address. Better to avoid the subject altogether.

His thoughts had been a complete jumble since he'd stepped out of her carriage. Their talk had been most revealing, and not only because he'd found out about that bounder of the worst sort, George Clayburn. She had also commented on their family, and he pondered her particular assessment of his attractiveness to women. He had dismissed it with some mild teasing, but it was true that he'd never lacked a dance partner, and he was well aware that there were more than a few women who considered him a prime match. But he'd never met a woman he was particularly drawn to, mostly because their intentions were highly transparent. They liked the idea of being with him, but they never seemed interested in getting to know him. Many a time he saw a young woman's eyes glaze over when he spoke of his travels. They seemed to have few interests outside of what went on in their narrow, superficial sphere.

He wanted something deeper, more meaningful. That was something he and Lily definitely had in common.

"Colin, could you pay attention to me for at least two minutes?"

"Sorry," he said, giving his sister his full attention, only to receive her dagger-filled glare. He cleared his throat. "You were saying?"

"I was saying that you are leaving again." Diana sighed. "You've only just returned from Scotland."

"Wanderlust is difficult to cure." He didn't offer any further explanation as he reached for the morning paper. Diana stopped him.

"I think you're running away."

Colin brushed her off. "From what?"

"I don't know. Why don't you tell me?"

He didn't reply, mostly because he wasn't sure what to say. Was he running away? And if he was, from what?

"Very well, if you insist on being secretive," she sniffed. She folded her linen napkin and set it on top of her still-full plate. "I am only your sister."

"Guilt will get you nowhere."

"It always works with Mother."

"That's true. But then, she's raised it to an art form."

Diana let out a small giggle. "I wonder if she's using it on Emily this morn."

"Why do you say that?"

"Well, it seems Mother has given up on you and I marrying anytime soon. Which pleases me to no end, I must admit. Until Emily started the Season, Mother had been rather overbearing about the whole thing, urging me toward one available gentleman after another. Always mentioning their strongest qualities—at least the ones *she* felt were important. Of course they were rarely the qualities I found intriguing. So now she has a new target in our fair sister." Diana's eyes sparkled with mirth. "And you will never believe who her prime suspect is?"

"Who?"

Diana grinned with glee. "Mother has decided that Emily and Michael are most suited for each other."

"Michael who?"

"Michael Balcarris, you dolt. Who else?"

Colin let this bit of news sink in. Now this was quite a surprise. He smiled. Then chuckled. Then burst into a hearty laugh. "Has Mother lost her mind? Emily and Michael? She practically loathes him."

"I know. They used to be so close when we were growing up. I guess Mother remembers how fond they were of each other back then and wishes for them to re-visit those feelings."

"But back then Emily was pest and Michael was . . . well, he was . . ."

"Manly?" Diana offered.

"You could say that. Now he's just plain odd. Emily will never stand for a match with him." Colin grinned at the ridiculousness of it. "Mother has her work cut out for her."

"That she does." Diana smiled in return. "And how fortunate for us she'll be spending all her energy con-vincing Emily that she and Michael are destined for each other. It will leave her little time to meddle in our love lives."

"I have no love life," Colin insisted.

"And why is that?" Diana asked. "You do realize you could easily have any woman you want, do not you?"

"I do not want to 'have' just any woman, Diana."

"So you are waiting for the perfect one? I didn't realize you were so picky."

"Not picky. Just discerning." Lily's image popped into his mind once more. Not just her image but her smile. She really had a lovely one. Why hadn't he noticed it before? And why was he thinking about her yet again, especially in a romantic context? Because while he was fantasizing about her mouth, the unexpected image of him kissing it entered his mind.

Now where had that thought come from?

"Colin," Diana said, her mirth disappearing, replaced by bewilderment. "Are you blushing?"

Blevins entered the room, saving Colin from having to answer, because much to his surprise, he was indeed blushing.

The butler carried a small silver tray laden with a generous pile of calling cards. He placed it near Diana, who immediately focused her attention on it. Colin said a prayer of thanks for the butler's brilliant sense of timing.

"Thank you," she said, pulling the tray closer to her. She thumbed through the cards. "This many already?"

"I am afraid so, my lady. The number of gentlemen callers seeking your company is increasing."

"Apparently so." She looked up at Blevins and smiled. "That will be all. I will send word when I am ready to receive visitors."

Blevins bowed and excused himself. Colin leaned back in his chair and folded his hands against his stomach. "You are enjoying this, aren't you?" he remarked, tilting his head in the direction of the cards.

"I do find it rather . . . pleasant. I guess we are different in that respect. You are overly discriminating, while I enjoy variety. Besides, it is all a bit of harmless fun." She picked up a card, read the name and set it down next to the tray. Selecting another one, she glanced at it and placed it next to the previous card. Colin watched for a few moments as she decisively went through the cards.

When she came to the last one, she glanced at it, then sighed. Her lips turned down in a slight frown. "Not again. Well, he certainly is persistent. I will give him that."

Colin grabbed the morning's paper and lifted it up. "Who?"

"Lord Tamesbury."

He peeked around the paper. "Gavin?"

She sighed again. "Yes."

He'd been so wrapped up in his own problems with Lily that he'd forgotten about Gavin's interest in his sister. Interest that apparently wasn't reciprocated, if her somber reaction was any indication. "Gavin's a fine chap, Diana. You should give the man a chance. He's thoroughly besotted with you."

"I know." She put the card back on the tray. "And I realize he's a good friend of yours, but . . . frankly, Colin, there's really nothing there."

"Nothing there?"

"How can I explain it?" She drummed her long, tapered fingers against the polished wood of the table. "He's handsome, charming, and highly intelligent."

"I fail to see the problem, Diana. It sounds like you two would be well suited."

"That's just it—we really should be. But I do not feel anything when we're together. No excitement. No anticipation. No *spark*. Not like I do with other men."

Colin put down the paper. "Exactly what are you doing with other men?" he asked sharply.

Diana laughed. "Nothing, of course. I am merely pointing out that Gavin, as sweet as he is, isn't the one for me." Removing her napkin from her lap, she rose from her chair. "I must be off, Colin. So much to do today. Ta." As Diana left the room, Blevins entered it.

"My lord?"

Colin looked up. "What is it, Blevins?"

"Lady Lily Breckenridge to see you, my lord."

"She is?"

"Yes, my lord."

This was most curious. He hadn't expected to see her here. "Are you sure she isn't here for Emily?"

Blevins shook his head. "She has insisted on seeing you."

Colin rose from his chair. "Tell her I will be right—"

"How could you?"

Lily stormed into the room, practically knocking over poor Blevins. He leaned against the doorframe for support, only to be knocked about again by Lily's maid.

"My lord, I tried to stop her," the maid said, panic etched on her face. "But she wouldn't listen to me."

Colin took a step back. He'd never seen Lily so angry. She radiated with it, her rage coming off of her in waves that threatened to tip him over. "Lily, what's wrong?"

"You know very well what's wrong. How could you betray me like this?"

"What are you talking about?"

"This!" She thrust the morning's newspaper at him, the paper crackling in her hand.

He read the front page headline, and blanched.

Chapter Thirteen

Lily fought for control, but she was perilously close to losing it. Her body shook, and had since she first saw the headline that morning. Fortunately her parents hadn't seen it. She could only imagine their reaction.

She watched with growing agitation as Colin finished reading the article. It was highly speculative and based on innuendo and heresay, but it was damaging enough.

When Colin finished reading, he lowered the page. "Lily, I promise you, I have no idea how they found out about Lady Thewlis' bracelet."

At least he had the good grace to look surprised. He even appeared a bit pale, as if he too was shocked. Not that it mattered. He was a bounder of the worst sort, especially after making her believe he was a man of

117

integrity. His planting the idea that she was the thief—in a public forum no less—only solidified his diminished stature in her eyes.

"Why did you do it?" she asked, struggling to keep her voice steady. She refused to fall to pieces in front of him. "Was it because of Michael?" He started to speak, but she interrupted him. She would have her say. "You picked the perfect revenge, I will give you that. Embarrassing me and my family in front of the entire *ton,* making everyone suspect that I am a criminal. I do not think even George would have gone that far." A lump formed in her throat, and despite her effort to keep it from happening, her eyes moistened.

"My lady?" Hannah said.

Lily whirled around. She had forgotten Hannah was there. She couldn't very well talk about this in front of her. And the last thing she wanted was to have her mother and father find out what was going on. Taking a deep breath, she fought to stem her emotions. "Hannah, I need to speak with Lord Chesreton right now. In private."

Hannah opened her mouth to protest, but then clamped it shut. "Yes, my lady." Turning on her heel, she left the room. But Lily knew she wouldn't stray far, and she suspected Hannah would be lingering right outside the door.

Colin tossed the paper aside and crossed the room. "Lily, listen to me. I had *nothing* to do with this. And to think I would stoop to something so low out of some twisted revenge over that business with Michael, that doesn't make any sense.

His argument punctured a hole in her bluster. "But, you are the only person who knew about the bracelet."

"Yes, but I never breathed a word of it to anyone." He moved toward her, closing the distance between them. "I would never betray you, Lily," he said softly, his voice barely above a husky whisper. "Ever. You have to believe that."

His image blurred in front of her. Blast it, she was near tears again, only this time they were tears of relief. He always seemed to see her at her most vulnerable.

"We'll find out who did this," he said, appearing as offended about the article as she was. "I promise you that."

She believed him. His sincerity was clear, in his eyes, his tone, everything about him vibrated with truth. She realized now she never should have doubted him. She felt like an idiot for doing so. "I am—"

He put his finger on her lips. "Apology accepted." Then he did something most unexpected—he slowly ran his fingertip across her mouth.

A shiver coursed through her, but she didn't pull away. She held her ground, waiting to see what he would do next. His gaze held hers as his finger trailed down her cheek and lightly outlined her chin before he drew away.

He shook his head slightly as if he were regaining his senses. Then he stepped back, breaking the invisible contact between them. "I . . ." He cleared his throat. "Gavin knows the owner of the paper. I will speak with him. You'll have a retraction by morning, I guarantee it."

"I appreciate that," she murmured, still mesmerized by what happened between them. Her mouth still tingled from his startling touch.

Suddenly he turned around and began pacing the breakfast room. He didn't look at her, instead focusing his attention on the measure of his steps. "Who could have done this?" he asked aloud. "And why?"

"I have no idea, Colin. Obviously I am clueless, since I first thought it was you."

He raised his brow, then resumed pacing. He seemed totally engrossed in wearing a path out on the gleaming waxed floor. "No one else was there in the foyer but you and I."

Taking his cue of ignoring the romantic moment that had just occurred—and it was most romantic indeed, enough to send chills throughout her body, even though she wasn't the least bit cold—she replied, "There was the footman."

"I seriously doubt he noticed anything. Once I took your cloak from him, he went back to his post." He stepped in front of the window, both hands clasped behind his back. "First the bracelet mysteriously appearing in your wrap, then the bogus story in the newspaper." He turned and looked at her, his expression one of utmost seriousness. "There is one thing for certain, Lily—someone is trying to frame you. Of that I have no doubt."

Fear gripped her for the first time since all this happened. She had pretty much experienced every emotion imaginable over the past couple days, but oddly enough fear wasn't one of them. Until now. "But how? More importantly, why?"

"I have not a clue. Do you have any enemies?"

She shook her head. "None that I can think of. At least no one who would go to such elaborate lengths to discredit me."

"What about your father? He's powerful, rich, and highly connected. A prime target, to be sure."

Lily thought for a moment. "He's hinted at nothing wrong at home."

"Hmmm," Colin murmured. He crossed his arms over his chest. "But extracting your parents' involvement and your lack of ill-willed acquaintances, that leaves . . ." He didn't complete his thought.

"No one."

"What about your maid?"

"Hannah? She is the epitome of discretion. Besides, she does not know anything about it." Lily sighed deeply and gripped the back of one of the Dymokes' breakfast-room chairs. The situation seemed so hopeless. How could they possibly find out who was behind all this if they had no idea where to start?

"Do not lose heart." His words were kind and reassuring, but he still kept his distance. "Everything will be sorted out in the end."

Lily gave him a doubting look. "How can you be so sure?"

"Because you are innocent. We both know that. The scoundrel that perpetrated all this will get his just reward. Justice always wins out in the end."

His confidence comforted her, just as his touch had excited her. With a boldness she didn't know she possessed, she went to him. Lifting her hand, she touched his cheek lightly with her palm. His eyes grew wide with surprise, but to her delight he didn't move back.

"Lily," he said hoarsely. "I—"

"Colin!"

Emily's shrill, angry call shattered the moment. They jumped apart immediately, retreating to opposite sides of the room. Hannah immediately surged into the room as if she had been there all morning.

Lily felt light-headed, her pulse racing out of control. Heat suffused her face, so much so she almost couldn't bear to look at him. She had acted so brazenly, so forcefully, and yet it had all felt so *right*. Against her will she looked at him, stunned to see two red blotches on his face and something in his eyes. Was he angry with her? She would not blame him if he was. Then she stilled. No, it wasn't anger she saw there. It was something else, something that took her completely aback.

Desire.

Emily stormed into the room, a whirlwind of indignation. "Colin, if you had anything to do with Mother's shenanigans this morning, I promise you—"

"Emily," Colin said, his voice sounding shaky and strange. "Lily's here." He broke his gaze from Lily and turned to face his sister.

"Oh . . ." Pausing in the middle of her tirade, Emily looked first to Colin, then to Lily, then cast a quick glance to Hannah in the corner, then to Colin again. Her head tilted to the side and she frowned for a moment, a peculiar expression on her face. "Did I interrupt something?"

"No!" they both said in unison, even though Emily had interrupted something. What, Lily wasn't exactly sure. She also didn't know whether to be upset or grateful about it.

"Well, very good then. Have you been waiting long?" Emily asked, turning her attention back to Lily.

"I beg your pardon?"

"Normally I do not go shopping this early in the day, but Mother insisted. And now I know why." She looked to Colin again, ire sneaking back into her tone. "She was practically picking out my trousseau, I will have you know."

"Trousseau?" Lily asked, realizing Emily assumed she was here to see her. Unwilling to allow her to think differently, she pushed aside her near kiss with Colin and the issue of the Bracelet Bandit focused all her attention on her friend.

Colin held up his hands in surrender. "Emily, what you and Mother do on your shopping trips is no concern of mine. Now if you'll both excuse me." He moved toward the exit of the room, avoiding eye contact with Lily.

"But I have not told you the worst part," Emily sputtered, following him. "She wants me to marry Michael Balcarris!"

He didn't seem the least bit surprised by the news. "You know Mother. She gets a notion in her mind, obsesses about it for a while, then moves on to the next thing. Do not fret about it."

"I know, Colin, but I think she's really serious about it this time. She spent the entire morning waxing poetically about what a romantic pair we would be, childhood friends turned adult sweethearts." Emily winced. "Has she even seen him lately? Romantic isn't a term I'd apply to him. Not at all. And here's the worst of it— she sent me home so she could go speak with him and his *mother* about making a match!"

"Emily," Colin said, impatience edging his tone. "I cannot really talk about this right now." He finally turned around and looked at Lily, his gaze holding hers while he spoke. "I have another matter that needs my immediate attention." He snatched the paper off the table and left the room.

"Well!" Emily looked at Lily. "What could possibly be more important than a crisis in his own family? Because that's what this is, a crisis. And my brother, in his usual, irresponsible style, has abandoned me. Again."

Lily held back a tiny smile, and simply shrugged. She did feel for her friend's predicament. Everyone, save Elizabeth Dymoke and perhaps Michael himself, knew Emily detested the man. So the idea of her being matrimonially matched to him had to be Emily's worst nightmare. Now Colin had added insult to injury by leaving so abruptly.

But Lily couldn't help the warm sensations traveling through her because she knew the real reason he left. To help her. And in her estimation that made him quite heroic, no matter how put out Emily was with him at the moment.

With a sigh Emily grabbed Lily's arm and dragged her to the table, practically forcing both of them to sit down. "Perhaps it is for the best. I do not think he'd understand about Michael anyway, as he's a man and they do not exactly understand matters of the heart."

"That's a rather overarching statement, do not you think?"

"All right, I will amend it then. *Brothers* do not exactly understand matters of the heart."

Lily's own heart skipped a beat as she remembered her near embrace with Colin mere moments ago, and the way he'd hurried off to take care of the offending newspaper article. While she had no brothers with which to validate Emily's statement, she was quite sure that Colin Dymoke absolutely understood matters of the heart.

"Michael! Michael, darling! We have a visitor!"

Emitting a low groan, Michael threw his arm over his eyes at the sound of his mother's penetrating voice. It sliced through the door of his room as if the wooden slab were as thin as onion skin. Although it was midmorning, he was exhausted, having spent most of the night in the worst parts of London ferreting out information from several drunken sots in the city's most low-brow establishments. He hadn't returned home until dawn. Even then he had trouble falling asleep, as he often did. Unrelenting insomnia had plagued him for years.

"Michael, dear, did you hear me?" The countess' voice raised another decibel. He wished his mother were like normal ladies of the house, sending servants to fetch their family members. It would allow Michael a chance to let down his guard a little more often. However, Ruby Balcarris had always been a doting mother, and he never knew where she would pop up next.

"Michael?"

He grimaced, then replied in his most proper tone, "Ah, yes, Mother. Heard you loud and clear. I shall be down in a moment."

"Splendid. Please hurry, love. We do not want to keep Lady Chesreton waiting."

He lifted his arm from his eyes. Lady Chesreton? What was Emily's mother doing here? It was most unusual for her to pay them a call this early in the day, and especially since she and his mother had only just seen each other at the party two days ago.

Thrusting the brocade coverlet off his body, he rolled out of bed and scrubbed a hand over his unshaven face. With weary steps he dragged himself to the washbasin perched on a small mahogany table. Above it hung a square, gilded looking glass. It was larger than he really needed, but it maintained the illusion of a man filled with vanity. Glancing at his reflection, he grimaced. He looked a wreck, his eyes puffy and red-rimmed, the dark, stubbly beard shadowing his chin. He grabbed a straight razor and began shaving with smooth, practiced strokes. Fortunately he had his toilette and dressing routine down to an exact science and could practically complete it in his sleep, which he was pretty much doing at the moment.

Twenty minutes later he emerged from his room the epitome of the English dandy everyone thought him to be. No one would have guessed he'd spent the dark hours consorting with common thieves, swindlers, and prostitutes. No one would have guessed his real occupation—a spy for the crown.

"Lady Chesreton," he exclaimed when he reached the drawing room. Bowing low, he executed a perfect leg. "What brings you to our, ah, humble home?" He gave her hand an airy kiss.

"Oh, Michael, you certainly are the charmer." Lady Chesreton giggled like a schoolgirl, and Michael grinned in return. He saw so much of fair Emily in the buxom blond, the daughter favoring the mother in appearance, if not temperament. While Lady Chesreton was easily swayed by flattering words and undivided attention, Emily barely abided it. At least she did when the words and attention were coming from him.

His smile faltered, but he quickly rebounded. He assumed the reason for Lady Chesreton's visit had to do with Colin. Perhaps she had also seen the troubling article in the newspaper this morning regarding Lily.

"Chocolate, dear?" His mother held up a delicate china pot he had brought home from the Orient. Fine tendrils of steam wafted through the tiny opening in the spout.

"Of course." He didn't particularly care for hot chocolate, but his mother had been serving it daily since he could remember. And playing the dutiful son was a necessary, if somewhat stressful, part of his role.

Once the ladies were seated on the soft, cushioned chairs, he followed suit and sat down on the settee, trying not to wince as the corset cut into his circulation. He crossed his leg over the other one at the knee. "May I inquire as to why you've decided to grace us with your lovely presence, my lady?' Michael asked, taking the teacup from his mother. He brought the drink to his lips.

"To speak to you about marrying Emily."

Michael nearly spat out his chocolate. It was only by sheer will that he managed to swallow the thick, sweet beverage at all. "Emily and me?" he said, nearly choking on both the chocolate and the words.

"Michael, are you all right?" His mother leaned toward him, her round face etched with concern.

"Fine, Mother." He brought his fist up to his mouth and coughed, then set the cup down on the small table in front of them. "Just went down the wrong way, that's all."

"You should drink more slowly next time, love," Ruby admonished.

"Yes, Mother." Michael turned to back to Elizabeth. "Lady Chesreton," he said once he regained his composure. "Did I hear you correctly? Regarding Emily and me and . . ." He gulped involuntarily. "Marriage?"

"I know this seems out of the blue," she began.

"Quite," he couldn't help saying, still reeling from the shock.

"But I simply cannot think of a more perfect match for my youngest daughter."

About a dozen men far more suitable for Emily than he was ran through Michael's mind, but he remained silent. Emily Dymoke needed a husband who was stable, one who was matrimonially minded. One who would be there for her when she needed him, not off sneaking away at night on secret missions and getting involved in intricate intrigue. What she did *not* need was him.

Even if he did love her to distraction.

The mere idea of marrying Emily, nay, of simply holding her in his arms as he had yearned to do for the past two years, and not during a stiff dance or *pas de deux* but as a man embracing the woman he loved, nearly undid him on the spot. It was something he had longed to do, and had dreamed of for a very long time.

But he couldn't dwell on what could never be, or what he desired more than anything. He had chosen his path. He had learned to stifle his own wants and emotions, to treat them as negligible and inconsequential. His life

didn't include marriage, or even female companion-
ship. And, mournfully, it would never include Emily.

In an effort to mask his thoughts, he let out an overly
bright laugh. "My dear Lady Chesreton, you do make
me chuckle. Emily and I? A couple?" He laughed
again, wiping away a fake tear. "Do forgive me, but
that's the most preposterous idea I've ever heard."

"Michael!" his mother chastised. "Do not be rude."

"Oh, I am truly sorry. But I cannot help it. This is all
so . . . amusing." He looked at the shocked and almost-
offended expression on Lady Chesreton's face, and realized his reaction was having the desired effect.
"Please, I meant no umbrage. Emily is a delightful
young lady. But I am afraid she's not, how should I put
it . . ." He glanced up at the ceiling as if in deep thought
before returning his focus to Emily's mother. "Well, to
be quite honest, she's hardly my type."

"Oh?" Lady Chesreton visibly bristled. "And exactly
what 'type' are you looking for?"

"Someone more sophisticated, to be sure. And pret-
tier. Perhaps a bit thinner as well. She's a bit too plump
in the hips to be fashionable, I must say."

With each word he spoke, a tiny dagger drove
deeper into his heart. Every word out of his mouth was
a lie. He thought her perfect in every way, and her
voluptuous build only added to her attractiveness in
his eyes. Yet he couldn't say so, not even to her
mother, who he could tell was on the verge of giving
him a royal dressing down, if not an outright slap in
the face.

"I do not understand," Elizabeth said, pushing her shoulders back just as Emily always did when she was put out. "I just knew . . ." She placed her half drank teacup on the table and stood. "I am sorry I brought this up. I should have never come here."

Ruby rose from her seat, nearly losing her balance but quickly steadying herself, and rushed to her friend. "Elizabeth, please." She cast Michael a puzzled look. "I think you merely caught my son off guard. Even I must admit your idea is most unexpected."

"To say the least." Michael picked up his chocolate and sipped it daintily, maintaining a placid expression.

"So now you think my Emily isn't good enough for your son?"

"No, no. I didn't mean that—"

"I will take my leave now," she said with an indignant sniff. She turned and looked at Michael. "Before I do, I will have you know that my Emily is a beautiful, perfectly proportioned woman with a good head on her shoulders. Any man would be proud to have her as his wife. Good day, my lord." Whirling around, she left the drawing room.

"Elizabeth, please . . ." the countess moved to go after her, but turned to her son. "I do not know what's gotten into you," she said, looking distraught. "Your behavior is outright dreadful." Then she left to chase after Lady Chesreton.

Carefully setting down his cup, Michael rose stiffly from the settee and crossed the room. He looked out the window and watched while his mother placated her dear friend. He had hurt both their feelings, and had done a bang-up job of it.

It had killed him to do it.

But it had to be done. He couldn't drag Emily into his world any more than he could his own mother. Better for the entire Dymoke family to think he was a cad than to risk them getting too close to him.

Leaning his forehead against the pane of glass, he closed his eyes as loneliness flooded his soul.

Emily grabbed a leftover scone. She and Lily had dismissed Hannah a few moments ago. The young woman had left quickly and with great relief. "It is quite preposterous, do not you think, the idea of Michael and I. I can barely stand to be in the same room with him."

Lily thought about her run-ins with Michael, especially her most recent ones. For all his annoying mannerisms and snobbish ways, he wasn't all *that* bad. Certainly he wasn't as horrid as she had initially thought. He had agreed to keep her and Colin's secret regarding their supposed tryst, after all. And even though it wasn't really true, he had thought so and still agreed to maintain his silence. She could think of far worse men Emily could be paired up with. George, for example. And she would not wish that man on her worst enemy.

She considered taking one of the scones, but decided against it once she saw the exorbitant amount of clotted cream Emily slathered on it. Apparently the scone was as dry as it looked. "You are being a bit harsh concerning Michael, do you not think? I believe he's been nothing but kind to you."

Shaking her head, Emily bit into the scone, then licked at a tiny dollop of cream at the corner of her mouth. "No, I do not believe I am. He drives me positively insane. That Mother would think the two of us a good match is disturbing in the extreme. I cannot imagine why the thought ever popped into her mind." She looked at Lily, her blond brows furrowing. "You do not think she's becoming addled, do you? I know that happens to people of advanced age."

"I doubt it. She's hardly elderly, Emily."

Emily put the scone back on her plate. "You are right of course. Well, I intend to put these crazy notions of hers to rest, and soon. Because the only suitable match for me is Gavin Tamesbury." She sighed. "Now there's a most wonderful man."

Lily smiled at the dreamy expression on her friend's face. She was also struck by how much she and Colin resembled each other. Which led her to think of their near kiss—

"You will help me, won't you, Lily?"

Emily's words brought Lily out of her musings, which was probably a good thing since her musings were taking her places she wasn't necessarily prepared to go. "Help you do what?"

"Get Gavin's attention. Have not you been listening?" She leaned back in her chair and clasped her fingers together. "Somehow I have to make him see how perfect I am for him."

"How do you propose to do that? Other than with your overabundant humility, of course." Lily smiled. She wished she had her friend's confidence.

"I am not sure. Which is why I need your help."

"I do not know how much help I could be. Considering my experience with George—and my nonexperience with anyone else . . ."

"George is a piffle-headed butter brain."

Lily laughed and grasped Emily's hand. "Yes he is, isn't he? Thanks so much for that. I've found so little to laugh at lately."

Sudden concern popped across Emily's features. "Why? Is something wrong?"

Lily realized she had said too much. Backpedaling quickly, she said, "No, everything's fine. Right as rain, it is."

Emily looked at her doubtfully. "You would tell me if there was something wrong, would you not?"

Emily's earnest words tore at Lily. She had to tell her about the Bracelet Bandit. She would eventually discover it from the paper anyway. And if not from that source, then from the wagging tongues of the *ton*. Besides, she didn't want to keep secrets from Emily. That would not be fair to her or their friendship. Keeping secrets never failed to cause a myriad of problems.

But what of Colin? He was an even bigger conundrum. Could she admit to Emily that she had started falling for him, especially when she could barely believe it herself? She wasn't sure she could. What would be the point, really, when she doubted he felt the same way. A man like him didn't fall in love with someone like her. It simply wasn't done.

It simply wasn't fair, either.

Lily rose from her chair, her emotions jumbled. She couldn't talk about any of this right now, not even with Emily. "You are such a dear," Lily said, embracing her tightly and focusing the topic back to her. "I will be happy to help you with Gavin any way I can."

"Superb. I will let you know when I've hatched my scheme, er, plan." Emily grinned. "Poor man won't know what hit him."

Lily grinned. "I am sure he won't. Poor man indeed."

"Emily! Emily—where are you?" Elizabeth Dymoke's voice echoed throughout the front of the house.

"In the breakfast room, Mother," Emily called out. She looked at Lily, who shrugged in reply.

The sound of a door being slammed caused both women to flinch. Emily stood as her mother came barreling into the room, much like Emily had precisely thirty minutes before. The older woman's face was flushed with anger. She looked like a teapot about to blow.

"Consider Michael Balcarris crossed off your list of suitors," she told Emily. "I do not want that dreadful excuse of a man anywhere near you." Before her daughter could reply, Elizabeth spun around and stormed out of the room.

"Well," Emily said after a long silence. "What do you make of that?"

"I've not a clue," Lily said. "But I would say your problem with Michael is solved, would not you?"

"Quite."

They turned and looked at each other, then burst into hearty laughter.

Chapter Fourteen

Colin didn't know what hit him, but it had him completely out of sorts.

The cloudy morning had given way to a partly sunny afternoon as he made his way to Gavin's flat to talk to him about getting that preposterous article retracted. It was perfect weather to take a walk and clear one's thoughts, so he had eschewed Blevins' offer to bring around the curricle. But although the weather was co-operating, his mind wasn't.

He had assured Lily that everything would turn out all right, despite not knowing if it would. With her featherlight fingertips touching his cheek, her luminous eyes darker than he'd ever seen them before, and the open and vulnerable expression on her face . . . he would have promised her the moon, the stars, and the exchequer if she had asked him to. But now, away from her and deeply mired in the reality of the situation, he didn't know what to do.

He pondered over the events of the past few days. He'd gone from barely knowing Lily to nearly kissing her in the span of a few days. He'd also become deeply entrenched in the mystery of whoever was framing her. But those weren't the things that astonished him the most.

He liked her. A lot. And he was attracted to her as well. Just being near her excited him. It didn't make sense. If someone had lined up all the available ladies of the peerage in front of him and forced him to make a choice, she would have been the last woman he would have picked.

But why?

Slowing his steps, he thought about that. Why hadn't she captured his attention before this? Had he been too distracted by the more flamboyant women of the *ton*? They easily caught the eye, but like a sunset, they faded to the beholder. Lily had been easily overlooked. Was he as shallow as most of the other gents in society? He feared that he was.

Shallow, aimless—those words described him perfectly. He was tired of it. Tired of living his life without a purpose, weary of his lack of direction.

It was far time he changed that.

Lily broke the seal on the folded piece of paper, read its contents and sighed heavily. An invitation to yet another party. Her fourth one this week. She had already agreed to attend the Treadway party tonight, despite her misgivings. She tossed the invitation aside. Despite the paper's retraction two days ago—Colin had been true to his word and had the paper not only retract its false story, but print an elaborate mea culpa that had teetered on excessive—she was still the talk of the town and the gossip and intrigue hadn't died down. Since the original article ran insinuating she was a thief, Lily had never been so popular in her life. Of course the peerage wasn't terribly interested in her witty banter or splendid sense of humor. She was merely fodder for their entertainment until some other scandal came along.

Three hours later she arrived at the Treadways', along with her designated chaperone for the night, her cousin Lady Rebecca, who instantly went to the refreshment table once they arrived. Lily barely had a moment to take in the wonderfully decorated hall when Colin appeared in front of her.

"May I have this dance?"

Before she could reply, he swept her up in his arms and whisked her on the floor. Yet despite his antics, his expression wasn't playful. It was dead serious. "Colin? Is something wrong?"

He took a deep breath, but still didn't speak. Finally, after hesitating far longer than Lily thought was normal, he said, "I suppose I should just come out with it."

"Come out with what? Colin, you are worrying me."

He looked away for a brief second, then back at her, his gaze boring into hers. "Lily . . . do you think I am shallow?"

Chapter Fifteen

Colin felt like an idiot the minute the words were out of his mouth. He had spent all day wondering if he should go to the party tonight, after finding out from Emily that Lily would be in attendance. He never liked these types of social gatherings, but he needed someone to talk to. Normally he sought out one of his sisters or Gavin, but this time he bypassed them all and went straight to Lily.

He wasn't quite sure what to make of that.

Lily gaped at him. He shouldn't have been surprised at her reaction. Not many women have men fling them out on the dance floor only to ask them such a ridiculous question. He watched as Lily opened her mouth to speak, then snapped it shut again. This led him to give a hasty explanation for such an off-putting question.

"I've been giving it a lot of thought the past couple

of days. Taking inventory of my life and accomplishments, if you will." He maneuvered her deftly around a corner. "And I realized, to my chagrin, that I have very little to recommend me."

"Colin, I—"

"I also thought about what you said the other day in the carriage, about things being easy for me and my sisters," he continued. "I can see why you would think that, because on the surface it seems so. And that led me to the conclusion that people really only see the surface, do not they? They do not take the time to see past the exterior into one's soul. Which got me thinking, what if someone took the time to look beyond *my* surface? What would they see? They would not see much. Of that I am certain."

"Colin, that's not true."

"Isn't it? Look at me, Lily. I am a shell of a man. A handsome one in some people's estimation, but nevertheless a shell. And when the shine wears off there'll be nothing but an empty vessel covered in tarnish."

"Oh, of all the ridiculous, overly dramatic things to say."

"Lily, I really think—"

"Now listen to me," she said, looking him straight in the eye. "I have no idea what precipitated this foray into self-pity, but it must stop. You have no idea how preposterous you sound." He started to speak again but she cut him off. "First of all, you are not a 'shell' of a man. You are a kind, utterly charming fellow who adores his family. An empty shell would not be capable of such depth."

"Thank you for that," he said quietly.

The music stopped playing, and they halted their steps. "Colin, this isn't like you. What happened?"

He let out a long sigh. "I am not sure. I think it is a combination of things. The other day Diana accused me of running away."

"From what?"

"I do not know. Which is the problem." He escorted her off the floor. "I do not have a clue about anything, it seems. But I've felt like this for a long time. Ever since my father died, actually. Did you know he was a lawyer?"

"No."

"He was, and an excellent one. He was also a brilliant businessman, and a terrific father. The man was perfect."

"No one's perfect, Colin."

"Well, he was as close to perfection as one could get. He often talked of us working together. He wanted nothing more for me than to join him in the profession."

"And what did you want?"

Colin shrugged. "Honestly, it had never really occurred to me that I'd be anything but a lawyer. So I went to school and studied law."

Lily's brows lifted in surprise. "So you really are a solicitor?"

Colin shook his head. "No. I found it excruciatingly boring, so I never finished the schooling. I graduated, but barely, and in a different discipline entirely. Besides, I was never very good at it. My marks were poor, so that didn't help any. To his credit my father never said anything overly harsh about it, but I knew I had disappointed him. Now he's gone and I cannot do anything to rectify that I failed him."

She regarded him for a moment. "Tell me, Colin, what are your hopes and dreams? What do you want from life?"

"I wish I knew. I've thought about it. A lot. But I have not come to any conclusions yet." He looked at Lily. "I am twenty-one years old, Lily, and I have no idea what I want to do. Or what I should do." He looked away. "I am sure I sound pathetic."

"Not at all," she said softly.

He faced her again. "I do know what I *do not* want to do, and that is spend the next five or six years of my life going to parties like these." He gestured to the crowded room with contempt. "I'd probably perish from boredom." He paused. "I envy you."

She looked genuinely shocked. "I believe that's the first time anyone's ever said that to me."

"It is true. You seem to know exactly what you are about."

"Oh, Colin, you are not the only one uncertain of the future. At one time, for a short while, I thought I knew exactly what life held for me."

"When you were with George," he supplied.

"Yes. But now . . . I just do not know. But I think this is all a part of finding our way in life. It would be easier if we were all born knowing what to do. But it doesn't work out that way."

"So we are basically struggling with the same thing?"

"I suppose so. We're just struggling in different ways."

He gazed at her for a moment, noticing once again how close in height they were. His eyes were level with hers, and he was mesmerized by their dark hue, stark against the creamy paleness of her skin. With every breath he took he inhaled her scent, a flowery combination he couldn't define. Her beauty, her sweet spirit and giving soul—everything about her stirred something deep inside him.

"Lily?" he whispered, suddenly losing all control of his rationality.

"Yes?

"I want to kiss you. Right now."

She could hardly believe this was happening. Here she was, on the perimeter of the Treadways' ballroom, the area packed to the brim with people. Most certainly her chaperone was lurking somewhere close by while Lily was sharing a rather intimate moment with one of the most handsome and eligible men in London, even if he didn't think so. It briefly crossed her mind that this was all highly improper. It had to be because the thrilling sensations running through her were anything but proper.

Then suddenly he stepped away. "I should go," he said, clearing his throat. "I should go now." He turned to walk away from her. "But we will finish this . . . conversation . . . another time. If you are so inclined."

She understood what he was saying. His admission wasn't a slip of the tongue. He meant it. The thought thrilled her to her toes. She gave him a shy smile. "Yes. That would be lovely."

With a graceful movement he slipped back into the crowd, the milling collection of people never knowing that something infinitely more complicated and wonderful was going on with Colin and Lily than a simple dance at a party.

Chapter Sixteen

"Lily, I simply do not know what's gotten into my brother." Emily twirled the handle of her parasol in her hand. "He's acting most peculiar. Even more peculiar than usual, which is saying a lot."

She and Lily were taking a short afternoon walk near Hyde Park. Despite the sun beating down on them, it was a pleasant afternoon. One of the few they had left before the heat of the summer increased the stench of London until it became nearly unbearable to walk outside. At that point most of the gentry escaped to the country. Lily wondered if the Bracelet Bandit would do the same.

It had been nearly a week since her dance with Colin, and there had been no news of any other robberies. Perhaps all that unpleasantness was over, and the bandit had left the city.

But where did that leave her and Colin? He had asked to call on her again, but she hadn't seen him since. And now Emily mentioned he was behaving strangely. She didn't know what to think.

"Have you got any ideas about what's wrong with him, Lily?"

Lily nearly laughed at the tone with which Emily delivered her question. She made it sound as if Colin had a mysterious illness or something equally objectionable. But Lily had to admit she was intrigued. What had Colin been doing with himself this past week? She knew what she had been doing—thinking about him nonstop. She remembered his deep voice when he said he wanted to kiss her, and the buzzing euphoria that had accompanied the revelation.

"Did you sigh, Lily?"

She looked at Emily and blushed, then averted her gaze again. She really did need to work on hiding her feelings better.

They rounded a corner and headed directly toward the park. Emily lifted her parasol and let the rod rest on her shoulder. "Yes, you did. And it sounded like a pleasant sigh, if I am not mistaken." Emily's eyes suddenly grew big, a knowing gleam sneaking into them. "Do you have a new suitor?"

Lily chuckled nervously. "A new suitor? Me? Whatever gave you that idea?"

"Lily, you must admit you've been quite preoccupied lately. And I get the distinct feeling you are keeping something from me." She cut Lily a sharp look. "You aren't, are you? Because you know you can tell me anything. I'd like to think we are close enough that you would feel free to do so."

Lily inwardly cringed as guilt clawed at her. She was being most unfair to Emily by not telling her about the bracelets, or about Colin. The situation had become quite sticky and she didn't know how to fix it. She didn't want to discuss the Bracelet Bandit, especially since the cretin had seemed to disappear without a trace. Why bring the unpleasant topic back up again? And then there was Colin. She had no idea what she could say to Emily on the subject of her brother, especially since she didn't understand what was going on between them herself.

"That's interesting," Emily said, halting her steps.

Lily looked at Emily, then followed the direction of her friend's gaze. Carriages, hacks, curricles, and phaetons of all sorts and sizes crowded the park as many of London's inhabitants were taking in the lovely day. Despite the horde of people, horseflesh and vehicles, it was easy to spot the striking couple. Diana, resplendent in a lavender and pale blue confection, was seated next to a handsome man Lily didn't recognize.

"Is that Duncan McKenzie with Diana?" Emily queried aloud.

"Who is he?"

"I do not know much about him, except that he is a laird from somewhere in the Scottish Highlands. I do know he has been sending his card quite often to Diana. I just had no idea she was interested in him."

The laird's phaeton was at a standstill because of the heavy traffic, Emily and Lily had a clear view of him and Diana. In fact, they couldn't have seen them any more clearly had they been the only people in the park. The women watched as he leaned over and whispered something in her ear. She giggled, then patted his knee, letting her hand linger longer than convention allowed.

"Seems she is very interested," Lily commented.

Now it was Emily's turn to sigh. "It does seem that way. But then again, it is always that way for Diana." She gave Lily a somber look. "I did not want to mention this, but I found out, quite by accident, that Gavin has been sending Diana his card too."

"Oh, Emily. I am so sorry."

"I am trying to be optimistic, because she definitely does not return his affections. She assured me of that."

"You spoke to her about your feelings for him, then?"

"Not exactly. It is quite embarrassing, you know, having the object of your affection giving his own affection to your sister."

Lily put her arm around Emily, her heart filled with compassion for her friend. "Let's go home," she said, urging her away.

Emily finally complied, but not until the vehicles started moving again, obscuring Diana from view. Her shoulders slumping, Emily said, "I know it is not her fault that everyone falls in love with her. But it is so unfair! There is only one man that I want, and he does not even know I am alive." Tears squeezed out of her eyes. "Oh, botheration! Now look who's here."

Lily peered up to see Michael Balcarris walking toward them, a crystal-topped walking stick in his hand. He was particularly overdressed today, with a brightly patterned waistcoat made of silver, opal, and gold fabric. The metallic threads reflected the rays of the bright sunlight, nearly blinding her and Emily as he approached. His quizzing glass was adorned with a colorful peacock feather. The man truly didn't know the meaning of the word "excessive."

"Is there any way to avoid him?" Emily asked, straightening her hat. She lifted her parasol off the ground and tried to regain her poise.

"I am afraid not. At least not without appearing rude in the extreme."

"I am willing to risk it."

"Emily!"

"Oh, all right."

"Good afternoon, ladies," Michael said as he strolled toward them. He lifted his quizzing glass and peered at them. "A fine day for a walk, do not you think?"

"Yes, my lord," Lily replied. As Michael met her gaze, he gave her a perceptive wink. Despite herself, a blush heated her face. The last time she had seen him was the day after he had caught her and Colin in his garden. She had paid him a visit and spent quite a good deal of time explaining to him that there was nothing untoward going on between her and Colin. And now there seemed to be something between them after all.

"Emily, dahling," Michael said, bending stiffly to

peer at her closely. Any trace of his initial conviviality immediately disappeared. "Have you been . . . crying?"

"That's none of your business," she snapped. She tugged on Lily's arm. "Now hello and good-bye, Lord Hathery. Lily and I must be on our way. We have a lot to do and you are keeping us from doing it."

Lily turned around and shrugged at Michael as Emily continued to lead her down the street. Then he did something most unexpected. He started after them. But he'd only taken a few steps before coming to a halt. Still she was close enough to see an unusual and uncharacteristic expression on his face. Disquiet, mixed with genuine concern. But just as quickly the emotion disappeared, replaced by his usual disinterested look.

"Emily, wait." Lily stared at Michael for another moment, then rushed to Emily's side, putting his reaction out of her mind for the moment.

Two days later, after not hearing a word from Emily, Lily decided to pay her a visit. After a light breakfast of fruit and cream, she dressed and readied to journey to the Dymokes'.

"If you would let James know I am ready to leave," she told Spencer as he approached her in the foyer. "And have Hannah meet me by the carriage."

"Yes, my lady. Also, this package came for you." He handed her a small bundle wrapped in brown paper and tied with twine. Her name was written on the front of it, but nothing else to indicate the identity of the sender.

"Do you know who it is from?

Spencer shook his head. "A young boy delivered it. I had never seen the lad before. I will go fetch James for you."

"Thank you."

Once Spencer left, Lily pulled on the twine and untied it, then folded back the crinkled paper. She drew in a sharp breath as she the contents were revealed.

Three gemstone bracelets glittered in her hand.

Cloistered away in his bedroom, Michael dipped his pen into the inkwell, then meticulously made tiny slash marks on the parchment. He sat back and investigated his work with a discerning eye. The code was a simple but effective one. After adding a few more pen strokes to the paper, he let it dry, then sanded, folded, and sealed it closed.

A knock sounded at the door. Quickly he gathered his supplies, stuffed them into a teakwood box and shoved it underneath his bed with his foot. Grabbing his quizzing glass, he struck a languid pose. "Yes?"

"It is me, my lord," Clewes said.

Michael dropped the quizzing glass on his small writing desk and crossed the room. Opening the door, he motioned for his friend to come in. "Any news?"

Clewes nodded. "You were right to put her under surveillance. She received a package this morn."

Michael's eyebrow lifted. "Interesting. Do you know who from?"

"No, but shortly after she accepted the package she left the house. In a hurry. And she looked most upset."

"Where did she go?"

"The Dymokes', my lord."

Michael nodded. He stepped away from Clewes and went back to his desk. "To see Colin, I am sure. Which means our elusive bandit has struck again."

"It would seem so."

Michael thought for a moment. Events had taken an unexpected turn. It seemed he would have to involve Colin and Lily after all. He didn't want to do so, but it appeared he had no other choice. "Clewes, my carriage, if you please. I think it's time I spoke to Lily and Colin."

Chapter Seventeen

Colin headed downstairs to the breakfast room, his heart happy and his soul light. He even skipped over the bottom step. He hadn't felt this good in a long time, and he had Lily to thank for it. He realized over the past couple of days that he seriously wanted to explore a relationship with her. From her response to his ill-timed reveal of his desire to kiss her, he assumed she wanted to as well. That confirmation deleted any embarrassment he may have experienced from being less than cool and collected with her.

"My lord?" Blevins met him at the bottom of the stairs, carrying a folded piece of paper. "This arrived for you just now."

Colin accepted it. "Thank you." He would read it later. Right now he had his family to contend with, and it seemed to be splitting at the seams at the moment.

154

But whatever news the message held, it could wait until later. As he moved to shove it into his pocket, Blevins stopped him.

"You should read it now, my lord."

"I am in the middle of something, Blevins. Surely it can wait."

"I do not believe it can."

At the urgent tone in his butler's voice, Colin gave him an odd look. It was most unusual for his butler to insist upon anything. Immediately Colin unfolded the paper. Spasms of alarm pulsated through him as he read the words on the parchment, written in a shaky hand.

I need to see you. Now. Meet me in your stable. Lily

Lily paced back and forth in the small stable behind the Dymoke house. She had snuck over here undetected after receiving the bracelets, even managing to give Hannah the slip. She was anxious and eager to talk to Colin. But she couldn't risk running into Emily or the rest of his family, or alerting any of her own staff, so she chose this rather unorthodox meeting place. At least it was private, and no one would find her here. She was taking a great risk, but she had no choice. The sweet aroma of hay mixed with the tang of horseflesh nearly overwhelmed her, but she held her ground.

"Lily?" Colin's low voice reached her ears.

"In here."

A few seconds later he emerged inside the darkened stable. "I can barely see you," he said. The strike of flint echoed through the confined space and light filled the room. He lit a lantern and hung it on a peg, then strode toward her.

"Lily, what happened?" He stopped mere inches from her. "You look a fright. Are you all right?"

She nodded, unable to speak despite needing to tell him what was wrong. Relief flooded through her at the sight of him, and the concern etched on his face seeped into her heart. More than anything she wanted to collapse into his arms, to feel his embrace surround her, to pretend this nightmare wasn't happening. But she couldn't fall apart, not now. Not when she needed every wit she could gather. Steeling herself, she said, "These were sent to me a short while ago." She folded back the paper and revealed the bracelets.

Colin's brows flew up as he scrutinized the jewelry. "You have no idea who sent them?

She shook her head.

"Did Spencer remember who delivered the package?"

"No," Lily clutched the bracelets in her hand. "He said it was a young man, one he hadn't seen before."

"Probably hired just to give you these," Colin concluded. He looked at Lily, his blue eyes searching her face. "I hate that you are going through this."

She turned from him, her thoughts and emotions a jumble. "I have to go to the authorities, Colin," she said, a tremor sneaking into her voice. "I do not have a choice."

She heard him come up behind her. "I know. This is far more than we can manage ourselves."

Turning around, she faced him. "But what if they do not believe me? What if they remember that wretched article in the paper and think I am the thief? My reputation, my parents' reputation—everything will be in ruins."

"I won't let that happen," he said firmly. "I will accompany you and vouch for you, tell them everything I know. Certainly between us both we can convince them of the truth."

"I hope so. I do not know what I will do if we cannot."

He gazed at her for a moment, then reached for her hand. "I will make sure they do. Wait here while I have the groom prepare our hack. We'll leave shortly. You won't have to do this alone."

Her heart swelled with emotion for this wonderful man. She did have an ally in all of this. "Thank you."

"No need to thank me, Lily. We're in this together. We have been since the beginning. And I vow to see it through with you to the end."

A quiet, rustling sound from behind them suddenly captured their attention. Colin drew Lily to him and they both turned around. Fear clutched at her as a man entered the stable. He removed his hat and bowed. "Lord Chesreton. Lady Lily."

Lily froze as he said her name. Who was this man? She had never seen him before. He was tall, slight of build, and older, with strands of gray blending with the thinning black hair at his temples. His serious demeanor, while not unfriendly, still made her uneasy.

She inched closer to Colin until she was nearly pressed against him. He released her hand and slipped his arm protectively around her waist.

"I do not know who you are, sir, but you are trespassing on my premises. I suggest you get out before I throw you out."

The man appeared unmoved by Colin's threat, despite it being delivered with more venom than Lily had ever heard Colin use. "Allow me to introduce myself," he said calmly. "I am Clewes. Now you and Lady Lily must come with me."

"And why would we do that?" Colin asked.

Clewes' gaze bored into him. "Because you have no choice."

"Now see here—"

"Do you want to clear her name?" Clewes gestured to Lily. "Ah, by your expression I can see you do. Therefore you will both accompany me—no questions asked."

Colin turned to Lily. "Do you know this man?"

She shook her head. "I've never seen him before in my life."

"But how does he know—"

"Lord Chesreton. We do not have much time."

Lily leaned forward and whispered in Colin's ear. "Do you think it is a trick?"

"I do not know. But he knows about the bracelets. For that reason alone we shouldn't cross him." He turned back to Clewes. "Where are we going?"

"No questions," Clewes repeated, then spun around. "Just follow me."

Lily and Colin trailed behind him as they left the stable. Lily felt Colin reach for the packet of bracelets in her hand. He took them and quietly slid them in his pocket.

She realized the magnitude of the gesture. If they were caught by the authorities, or anyone for that matter, he would have the bracelets on his person, thereby casting suspicion on himself. When she met his gaze, he responded with a small smile.

Clewes led them to a small black carriage that possessed no identifying marks on the outside. It was parked a few feet from the Dymoke house. Opening the door, Clewes motioned for Colin and Lily to go inside.

Lily and Colin exchanged doubtful looks. He took her hand and helped her into the carriage, and then clambered in behind her. The door immediately shut behind him, plunging them both into the darkness of the vehicle.

Then Lily felt something cover her mouth. Fabric of some kind. Her body stiffened as the cloth pressed against her nose, blocking her ability to breathe. She thrashed against it, gasping for air, until consciousness slipped away . . .

Chapter Eighteen

Colin struggled to open his eyes, but the lids felt heavy and sticky. With great effort he managed to open one of them to a small slit. He tried to lift his head, but he couldn't move it very far, since it felt as if a heavy boulder were attached to his neck. He lay back down again, shutting his eyes to keep the room from spinning.

A few moments later he tried again. This time he was able to open both eyes. He blinked, then slowly reached up to rub the grittiness away with his fingers. Where was he? The ceiling above him didn't look familiar and at the moment that was the only thing he could maintain his focus on. He worked to clear his fuzzy brain, trying to sort out the confusion plaguing him. Images fleeted across his mind. Being with Lily at the stable. The strange man Clewes. The bracelets that were delivered to Lily's house. . . .

His hand went to his pocket. The packet was still there. He could feel the hard stones of the jewelry through the wool fabric of his jacket. Breathing out a sigh of relief that the jewels were still safe, he forced himself to a sitting position, ignored the dizziness, and scanned his surroundings.

He was in a bedroom of some sort, and had been lying prone on a large bed on top of an opulent brocade spread. A spike of pain shot though his head, and he leaned back, making contact with an ornate wooden headboard. The bedroom was well furnished, and he realized that other than the groggy ache assaulting his head, he was quite comfortable.

But where was he? And where was Lily?

Swinging his legs over the side of the bed, he then stepped on the floor. Yet when he put weight on feet, his knees buckled.

"Careful, my lord. It will take you a little while to regain your equilibrium."

Colin turned to see Clewes entering the room, his irritatingly calm, unflappable expression firmly in place. Frustration pulsed through him. "What in the blazes is going on here? And where's Lily?"

"I assure you she's fine, my lord." Clewes walked over to Colin and reached out to assist him to a standing position.

Colin shook off the man's help, even though he probably could have used it, as he was still quite wobbly. "She had better be, or you will regret it. I want some answers, sir, and I want them now."

"In due time, my lord. All in due time. However, I know this has been most trying for you. I apologize for the inconvenience,"

"Inconvenience? You call kidnapping an inconvenience?"

"There was no other way to get you and Lady Lily here. Discretion is of the uppermost importance."

Scooting off the bed, Colin's feet hit the floor again. "Where exactly is here? And where are my boots?"

"Right here, my lord." Clewes walked to the end of the bed and handed Colin his black boots. Colin tried to yank them on, only to lose his balance and fall back on the bed. He stifled a groan of frustration. He would not let this man know how off-kilter he really was.

"Slowly, my lord. You must do things slowly." Clewes put his arm around Colin and helped him to a standing position. "There you go. Now, if you'll come with me—"

Colin shrugged him off. He was beyond annoyed with this man. "I am not going anywhere until I get some answers. I do not know what kind of game you are playing, but it has to stop now."

Clewes expression hardened. "This isn't a game, my lord. I assure you of that."

"Where is Lily? What have you done with her?" Colin clumsily made his way to the door, determined to find her. But Clewes blocked his path.

"As I stated before, she is fine."

"I want to see her."

"And you will, my lord. But the chloroform we used

on both of you is very potent, and takes time to wear off. Lady Lily hasn't awakened yet."

Alarm shot through him. "We? Who are you in cahoots with? Blast it, man, tell me what's going on!"

"Lily . . . Lily."

Lily's head throbbed as she opened her eyes to the blurry image of a man standing over her. He reached out and gently touched her shoulder. "Lily?"

"Colin?" She blinked a few times to clear her vision. She placed her palm over the man's hand. But just as their flesh touched she realized he wasn't Colin. Quickly she snatched back her hand, completely unnerved.

As his image began to clear, she realized she didn't recognize him, which only added to her trepidation. He was dressed in a simple white shirt open at the neck, and slim black trousers. His brown hair was as disheveled as the rest of his appearance, and he sported a day's growth of beard. Continuing to examine him, she finally realized who he was.

"Lord Hathery?"

He nodded, his expression one of utmost seriousness.

"What are you doing here?" She glanced around the room for a moment, trying to gain her bearings. "What am *I* doing here? And where is *here* exactly?" She tried to sit up, but became light-headed. "Where is Colin?"

"Here, allow me." Michael put his hand underneath her arm and helped her to a sitting position. She had been reclining on a couch of some sort, and another quick scan of the room revealed she was in a study.

Bookshelves lined the room, and she saw a large desk positioned on the opposite side. Who owned the study she had no idea. In fact she understood very little of her situation. She was still trying to figure out why her head hurt.

"I know you have a lot of questions," Michael said, reading her mind as if he had crawled directly inside it. "And you'll get your answers as soon as possible. But I wanted to speak with you, privately. Regarding a personal matter." He sat down at the opposite end of the couch.

"Michael, I . . . wait." She regarded him for a moment. "Where is your quizzing glass?" She looked him up and down, taking in his unusual appearance. Actually his appearance wasn't that unusual, for a normal man. But as everyone knew, Michael was far from normal. "And your cravat? Did you know your shirt is *open*?"

His hand went up to his collar. "Sorry about that," he said, but made no move fasten the buttons. In fact he barely seemed to notice his state of undress. "Lily, I do not have much time. Colin will be here in any moment—"

"Anything you have to say to me you can say in front of Colin. We have no secrets between each other."

"I am glad to hear that, because secrets can be most bothersome. Take it from someone who knows. But I cannot speak to you in his presence, not regarding this." He took a deep breath. "It is about Emily."

"Emily?"

"She was clearly upset the other day in the park.

Has something happened? Is she okay? She's not hurt, is she?"

Lily tilted her head to the side, confused by his sudden concern for her friend. "Michael, what is all this about?"

He leaned forward, his eyes filled with intensity. "Lily, I need to know if Emily is okay."

The insistence in his tone took her aback, along with his serious expression. This wasn't the Michael she was used to seeing. Gone was the snooty tone, the arrogant posture, the vain countenance. An earnest man sat beside her, asking about Emily with great concern. Although she didn't know why he had this intense concern, she had to answer his question. Not to reply to such sincerity would be cruel in the extreme. Still, she was wary. Emily would not appreciate Lily spilling her personal business, especially to Michael Balcarris.

"She's . . . all right," Lily finally admitted.

"Lily, please. Whatever you tell me I will keep in strictest confidence, I promise you. I would never betray Emily. Has someone hurt her?"

His correct assumption surprised her. "How did you know?"

"I didn't, not for sure. But I suspected as much." He raked his hand through his hair, and for the first time Lily noticed how tired he looked. Beyond tired, actually, he looked positively exhausted. "Who is he?" he asked, staring straight ahead.

"Gavin Parringer, Lord Tamesbury. But Michael, I do not believe he meant to hurt her feelings, not on purpose. From what I know he is a decent man. I am sure Emily would not adore him so much if he weren't. I am fairly certain he isn't aware of her affection for him. And unfortunately for Emily he seems to be quite taken with Diana."

Michael looked down on the floor, obviously lost in thought. "I see. So Emily has feelings for this man?"

"Yes, very deep ones." Ignoring her throbbing head, she moved closer to him. "But that is all I am going to say on the matter."

"I understand."

"Now, I have answered your questions, now answer mine. Why is her welfare so important to you?"

Michael hesitated, uncertainty creeping into his eyes as he looked at her. "I just needed to know how she was, that's all." He shot up from his seat, effectively ending her line of questioning. "I will go see what's keeping Colin and Clewes. And please, do not tell anyone we discussed this. Especially Emily or Colin."

Lily tried to stand, but Michael motioned her to sit back down. "Rest a little while longer, Lily. I will be back shortly." He turned and left the room with quick, long strides.

"Well, that was . . . confusing," she said aloud. In fact all of this was. She still didn't know what she was doing here, why her head hurt, and worst of all, where Colin was. She took a modicum of comfort from the fact that Michael was here, and seemed to know exactly what was going on. But his involvement didn't alleviate all her apprehension. And just who was that Clewes fellow, anyway?

Within a few minutes Michael returned, Colin and Clewes in tow. "You better have a good explanation for all this, Balcarris," Colin said as he followed the slightly shorter man. "Drugged, kidnapped—" he stopped talking as soon as he saw Lily. He crossed the room and sat down next to her. "Lily, are you hurt? Are you all right? They have not done anything to you, have they?"

"I am fine, Colin. You know Michael would not let anything happen to me." She was unable to hold back a smile. His genuine concern warmed her clear to her toes. "Are you all right?" He looked a bit rumpled but appeared unharmed.

"A touch of a headache," he said. "But other than that, no worse for wear." He turned to Michael, glowering. "Now, I've had enough of this silly cloak-and-dagger business. Michael, you've been acting strangely since your return from school, but this takes it all. By Jove, I better have an explanation and a good one, or I will have the authorities after you and your accomplice."

"No, you won't," Michael said evenly, seating himself in a plush green velvet chair directly across from them.

"And why not?"

"Because, my dear friend, I *am* the authorities."

Chapter Nineteen

Colin accepted the drink from Clewes' outstretched hand. As he sipped the warmed brandy, the fog that had covered his brain for the past few hours lifted. Yet perhaps there were some lingering effects from the drug, for he still wasn't sure if the Michael Balcarris sitting across from him was real or a figment of his hazy imagination.

Michael cupped his brandy in his hand, his palm cradling the bowl of the snifter, the stem between his fingers. He casually crossed one ankle over the opposite knee and leaned back in the seat, his arm draped over the chair back. But while his stance seemed relaxed, his eyes were highly alert. He no longer wore the bored, glazed look he so often sported. Instead it was replaced by a concentration Colin had never witnessed before.

Michael's gaze darted from Colin to rest on Lily. Only then did his expression soften a tiny bit as he continued to look at her.

Colin cast her a sideways glance. She sat next to him on the sofa and closest to the fire that Clewes had lit a few moments earlier. It bathed her in glowing warmth, the soft light caressing her face and brightening her dark brown eyes. He looked back at Michael, who was still gazing at Lily. A pang of jealousy tugged at him. Setting his brandy down on the table in front of the couch with a loud clink, he leaned forward. The abrupt noise had its desired affect, as Michael returned his attention to Colin.

"We've waited long enough, Balcarris," Colin said, his patience dried up. "Answers. Now."

Michael nodded. "Very well. I apologize it has had to come to this. I wish the circumstances were different." He took a long drink of his brandy, seemingly determined to drag this out as long as possible.

"I am not in the mood for your usual drama, mate. Just tell us why we're here—under rather criminal circumstances, I might add."

"I am afraid there was no other way. I couldn't risk you or Lady Lily discovering this place."

"What is this place, exactly?" Lily piped in.

"My refuge. It is where I conduct my most clandestine business."

Colin scoffed. "Exactly what kind of clandestine business would a foppish peer of the realm have?"

"A fop would not have any business at all." Michael

peered at him over the lip of his snifter. "But a spy would." He took another drink.

Lily gasped. "A spy? You?" She looked genuinely shocked.

If Michael was insulted at her incredulous tone, he didn't let on. "For the past decade I've been working for the crown, mostly overseas. Up until three years ago, that is, when my superiors needed my services here in London. They asked me to infiltrate the peerage, which proved quite easy since I myself am a member of the aristocracy."

"Which also explains your ridiculous clothing and airs," Colin said, realization starting to dawn. "I'd been wondering about all that nonsense. I couldn't fathom the Michael Balcarris I knew as a lad growing up to be Brummell's twin."

He grinned. "Really, Colin, did you actually think I would behave that way on purpose?"

"I will admit you had me stumped," Colin relaxed for the first time since they'd arrived. The man speaking to him now was the Michael he was familiar with. It was such a relief to know that he was faking being a vain dandy.

Michael's smile faded. "I've been able to keep my position a secret from everyone, with the exception of Clewes, who has been indispensable to me. And because of certain circumstances, you and Lady Lily are now privy to my secret. But I must implore you that what you learn here today can go no further than this room. Because if it does, not only will my life be in danger, but both of yours as well. I cannot stress this enough."

"You have my word, Michael," Colin said solemnly. "I will not speak a word of this to a soul."

"Neither will I," Lily added. She leaned forward on the couch, her eyes sparkling with delight. "This is so exciting! You certainly had me fooled. I would have never mistaken you for an undercover operative."

"Then my disguise was a success."

"Absolutely."

"And we must keep it that way."

"Oh, of course." She clasped her hands together. "So tell me, what is it like to live on the cusp of danger? To have your life filled with intrigue?"

"Lily," Colin interrupted. "Enough with the inquisition. I think we should stick with the business at hand, do not you?"

"Oh, yes." She leaned back, a little subdued. "I suppose you're right."

Colin fought a smile. Only Lily would see this situation as exciting. Truth be told, he found it exhilarating as well. He was also dying of curiosity as to why Michael chose this moment to reveal himself to them.

Michael set down the snifter and uncrossed his legs. "The reason I've brought you here is because I had no other choice. For the past three months I've been investigating the Bracelet Bandit."

"I knew it!" Lily jumped up. "I knew you were lurking in your garden that night. So you had seen the thief after all."

"Yes." Michael looked at her sternly. "But when you and Colin showed up, he was able to make his escape."

"Oh." Lily sat back down.

"And then I found you two snooping in my garden the next day. With your prowling around, that pretty much destroyed any chance of finding clues."

"Egad," Colin said. "Sorry, mate."

Lily also appeared contrite. "That was my fault. Colin tried to stop me . . . but I would not listen to him."

Michael looked at her, his mouth tipping in a half smile. "There's nothing we can do about that now. If there's one thing I have learned in this business, it is that nothing goes according to plan. Which leads me to why I've brought you both here. I need your help."

Colin blinked in surprise. "Our help? I would think our interference was the last thing you'd need."

"Or want," Lily added.

"On the contrary, I believe you'll both be valuable assets. And necessary ones." He turned to Lily. "Besides, my lady, you are already intricately involved. I fear that someone is aiming to besmirch you and your family."

She nodded. "I know. Colin and I have been trying to figure out who it is, but we have not come up with anyone yet."

"It is most puzzling," Michael said, "because for weeks the burglar was singularly focused on stealing the bracelets. Now he seems to have expanded his horizons."

"But why just bracelets?" Colin asked. "Why not

steal other valuables as well? There are far more expensive items to be taken in these homes than just bracelets."

"Because he's looking for one piece in particular." Michael rose from his chair and walked over to a small cabinet in the corner of the room. He opened the top drawer, withdrew a plain wooden box, then walked back to them. Handing the box to Lily, he said, "Open it."

Colin watched as Lily carefully unlatched the lid and pushed it up. She drew in a small breath. "It is beautiful."

"Take it out."

Lily removed a stunning, multicolored gemstone bracelet encased in a filigree gold setting. Amethyst, ruby, diamond, sapphire, and emerald jewels glittered and twinkled in the firelight. Each stone was cut in a different shape—square, diamond, round, octagonal. And each one weighed at least two carats. Even Colin had to admit it was one of the most stunning pieces he had ever seen.

She placed the bracelet on top of her wrist, letting the light catch the different cuts on the stones. "Why are you showing us this?"

"Turn it over."

Lily complied, carefully turning the piece over. She inspected it for a moment. "Colin, come take a look."

He stood and went over to Lily, leaning over her shoulder. Etched on the back of each stone was a tiny symbol, barely visible, along with something he didn't recognize. "What are these?" he asked, pointing to the ruby's etching.

"What you are holding is known as the Ruby Key. The symbols engraved on the back of the stone are part of a secret combination to a coffer containing documents that could bring down the British realm."

"You are joking." Colin laughed and looked at Michael, his mirth fading when his friend remained stone-faced. "That sounds preposterous. Like something out of a fanciful story."

"I agree it does, but it is also true. From our intelligence we've deduced that the bandit must be looking for this particular piece. He is aware of the existence of the code and that it is etched on a bracelet, but he's not sure on which piece of jewelry. Thus he's been pilfering the wealthy in search of it."

"But if that's the case, then why do *you* have such an important object? I would think the government would keep such a thing under very heavy guard."

"They do. The piece Lily is holding is a fake."

"But if it's under guard, then why would someone think the bracelet was in the possession of someone in the *ton*?"

"There have been several attempts to steal it," Michael explained. "But we have failed to find the perpetrator. By circulating information that the bracelet is somewhere in London, we hope to flush out the thief. The fake piece is the bait that will lead us directly to him." He stepped forward and clasped the bracelet onto Lily's wrist. "It looks lovely on you."

Colin suddenly realized what Michael intended to do. "You are not going to let Lily wear that in public."

"She must. We had hoped it wouldn't come to this, but the man is craftier than we had anticipated. Tomorrow the Duke and Duchess of Mantua are hosting their final ball before leaving for the country. It will be heavily attended. I have no doubt our thief will put in an appearance." He looked to Lily. "Especially if he knows you are in attendance. For some reason his intentions have gone beyond the bracelet and have included you."

"But I do not understand," Lily said. "My family has nothing to do with the government, other than my father's occasional visit to parliament. To be frank, he eschews politics. Not only does he think it frightfully boring, he doesn't like the cutthroat shenanigans that go on in those circles. He avoids the subject entirely."

"Then perhaps it is personal." Michael looked at her questioningly. "Maybe the thief is someone you know."

"Lily and I have gone over this already," Colin said, straightening. He moved in front of Michael. "What you are asking her to do is dangerous, and I forbid it."

"You what?"

Colin spun around to see Lily's face turn crimson, indignity contorting her features. "You *forbid* me to do this? May I remind you, my lord, that you do not own me."

Oh bother, she was back to spouting formalities again, a sure sign she was angry. "All right, I will admit to using a poor choice of words. But surely you understand how dangerous this is?"

"I am sure Lord Hathery will take precautions to see

that I am not in any danger." She peered around Colin's shoulder to look at Michael. "Right?"

"My colleague and I will do everything within our power to keep you safe. However, Colin is right. There is an element of danger. And I know I am asking a lot of you—of both of you, because I will need Colin to be there as well. Please, sit down, and I will explain." He gestured for both of them to return to their seats. When they resumed their places, he said, "We need to draw the thief's attention to the bracelet. Although I think once he sees Lily at the ball she will already have his attention. Therefore I am certain he will try to detain you in some way as to get the bracelet in his possession. He's already proven himself a skilled burglar, perhaps he's an excellent pickpocket as well. It is my hope he will ask you to dance."

"And what is my role in this?" Colin asked.

"To assist Clewes and I, along with a couple of our operatives. We must secure the area and keep our eyes on the guests. I will need someone to keep Lily under surveillance at all times. That is where you come in, Colin."

Colin thought for a moment. "I do not like this idea. Not at all. It is too risky for Lily."

"Colin—" Lily started.

He shook his head firmly. "I cannot let you do this." Rising from the chair he looked at Michael. "I am afraid you'll have to figure out some other way, mate."

"There is no other way."

"Why not just spread the word that the bracelet is missing? That it was stolen and sent to France or India or some other place?"

"Because we have him here in London, in close proximity. Once he leaves the city there will be little hope of catching him. We have been on his trail for the past year."

Michael's explanation made sense to Colin, but he wasn't in the mood to hear it. How could the man even think of putting Lily in harm's way like this? Even if it was to catch a burglar and save Crown secrets, it wasn't worth her getting hurt, or worse. "I still say no."

"It is not your choice to make." Lily moved next to him.

"I know what you are going to say. I am not changing my mind."

"You do not have to, because this isn't your decision. It is mine." She squared her shoulders. "I am going to help Michael, Colin, whether you agree or not. And whether you agree to help us or not."

"Lily . . . do not do this. What if something goes wrong? Michael just said the best plans can still go awry."

"I am not going to let fear keep me from doing the right thing. This man has terrorized the peerage. He has stolen from them, he has violated their homes and their personal possessions. He has tried to frame me for it. I want to see justice served." She moved a step closer to him. "Don't you?"

"Yes. But not at your expense."

"I will be fine," she insisted.

He really thought she believed that. He admired her bravery. But he couldn't stem the fear that this was a bad idea. "There has to be another way."

A shy smile played on her lips. "Lord Chesreton, if I didn't know any better, I would say you cared about what happens to me."

She might have been teasing, but he was dead serious. "I do care. Very much."

The teasing glint in her eyes faded, replaced by wariness. "Do not toy with me, Colin."

"I never toy, Lily. And not with something as important as this."

"Lily. Colin." Michael rose from his seat. "Time is of the essence. We mustn't dally any longer."

Lily nodded. "I will be happy to help you any way I can."

"But, Lily—"

"Can we count on you Colin, as well?"

Lily turned and waited for Colin's response. His face was grim, his mouth pressed in a thin line. He seemed on the verge of refusing. He glanced at her, giving her one last imploring look. She squared her shoulders and lifted her chin. Regardless of his answer, she was determined to help catch the burglar.

After a long moment, he broke their gaze and looked at Michael. "Yes. I will help you. But on one condition."

"What is that?"

"Once she arrives to the ball, I will not leave her side."

Lily's eyes widened. Did he understand what that type of constant attention would convey to society? "You cannot be serious."

"I am very serious. I will do everything I can to keep you safe, Lily." He held her gaze. "And I mean everything."

"But Colin," she said, hurrying to him. "Do not you realize what this means? People will think we are—"

"I do not care what anyone else thinks," he said resolutely. "My only concern is to keep you safe. That is my top priority."

Lily couldn't believe what she was hearing, that this was the same man who only two weeks ago was distraught at the idea of the two of them being linked together. Now he was willing to practically announce to the *ton* that he had designs on her. The mere prospect of it made her feel giddy inside. Yet the giddiness was tempered with the knowledge that he was doing this because he feared for her safety, and no other reason. It would all be a ruse, a necessary one in order to catch the thief.

"Very good," Michael said, seemingly not the least bit surprised at Colin's request. "I believe we will successfully apprehend this scoundrel with your help. Now, we must return to London proper before we are missed."

"And how do you propose to do that?" Colin asked. "Surely not by drugging us again."

"No," Michael said, approaching him. He held out two strips of black cloth. "Blindfolds."

"Is that really necessary?" Colin folded his arms over his chest. "I mean really, Michael. Of all the ridiculous, preposterous—"

"Colin," Lily said in a warning tone.

"I am afraid it is necessary." Michael handed him one of the cloths. "Would you put this on Lady Lily? Then Clewes will secure your blindfold, and lead you to the carriage. I will see you both at the party tomorrow." He turned and left the room. Clewes entered mere moments later.

A flash of annoyance crossed Colin's face. "This is absurd," he muttered. "Blindfolds?"

"I find it intriguing," Lily admitted, turning around.

"You do?"

"Yes. And very cloak-and-dagger, to use your terms." She leaned back, giving him nonverbal permission to blindfold her. "It is still quite hard to fathom, do not you think?"

"What is?" Colin asked, taking the cloth and placing it over Lily's eyes.

"Michael being a spy. I guess you could say we are spies too, as we will be helping to save the Crown."

"I would not go that far. I would say we are more like drafted infantry. It is not as if we had much of a choice."

She smiled at the softer tone in his voice. "I am glad to see you have come to terms with this so quickly."

"I have done nothing of the sort." She felt him secure the blindfold in place at the back of her head, tying it gently but tightly enough.

As Clewes blindfolded Colin, Lily thought about what she had agreed to do. For the first time ever she found herself looking forward to attending a ball. And Colin would be by her side, no less. It was the perfect plan to catch a thief. And with Colin and Michael looking out for her welfare, nothing could go wrong. Of that she was positively sure.

Chapter Twenty

"Colin, I have never seen you so agitated." Elizabeth brushed a few stray pieces of lint from her son's jacket as they stood in the foyer of the Dymoke residence. "There. You look as handsome as always. I think the teal and silver stripes in your waistcoat compliment you quite well."

"Thank you, Mother," he said absently. Tugging at his cravat, he struggled to stem the dread pooling inside him. He was also battling fatigue due to lack of sleep. Over the course of the last several hours he had tried to process everything that had transpired. Michael, his childhood friend, was a spy. And he was so good at it that he had everyone, including Colin, fooled. Thinking about Michael's successful public persona of a superficial fop, Colin thought the man had missed his calling. Michael would have been a genius on the stage.

And had he been an actor, he would not have had the opportunity to drag Lily into his dangerous plot.

The more he thought about it, the more he found Michael's plan to catch the Bracelet Bandit less and less appealing. He was highly irritated with his friend for involving them at all. The chance for error was high. And while Colin didn't fear for himself at all, he was nearly consumed with it for Lily. The thought of anything happening to her nearly tore him up inside.

"Colin, darling, will you fetch the carriage?"

He looked at his mother, who was dressed to impress in a ruby red gown with a lace overlay. He noticed the strands of gray threading through her light brown hair, and the tiny lines that appeared at the corners of her eyes when she laughed seemed more pronounced lately. Yet she was still one of the most beautiful women he knew. He pressed a kiss to her cheek.

Her white-gloved hand touched her face, her complexion suddenly flushed. "What was that for?"

"Because I love you. I am afraid I have not expressed it enough lately. I have been so wrapped up in myself these past months, and for that I am truly sorry."

Elizabeth smiled. "You have always been such a good boy—man," she quickly corrected. "A son any mother would be proud of. You are a kind, intelligent man who cares about others—about their feelings, about their welfare. That is what is important, sweetheart. There are too many cutthroat men in this world." She smiled.

Colin swallowed. At that moment he saw his mother

in a new light. Despite the outward appearance of a society maven, she was a watcher of people, a discerner of character. He reached for her hand. "Thank you."

Her face split into a grin. "Now, now, no need to thank me. I am only doing what every mother should do—nurture her child. Although I think we should talk more often."

"Absolutely."

She patted his cheek. "Grand. Then we will pick up this thread of conversation at a later time, for we will be dreadfully late for the party if we delay any further."

"About that," Colin said. "I must ask you a favor."

"Anything, darling."

"Please, under no circumstances, force me to dance with Carolina."

"But Colin, she'll be expecting you to dance with her. You always have in the past."

"I know. But I must confess that I have done it merely to be polite, not because I am interested in her."

"Well, although I've vowed not to interfere with your personal lives since that debacle with Michael Balcarris," she said his name as if he were no better than a bug squashed on the bottom of her shoe, "I still think you and Carolina make a striking couple. So one little dance with her cannot hurt now, can it?"

"It will if I am with Lily Breckenridge."

Elizabeth clasped her gloved hands together. "Lily? Why, I had no idea you fancied her so much."

"I do . . . I mean, I do not . . ." Oh, he was bumbling this magnificently. He couldn't even coherently come up with a suitable explanation without revealing his true purpose for being with Lily. So much for his future as a spy, not that he wanted one. But he could hardly admit to his mother how much he cared for Lily. At least not right now, for she would ply him with a thousand questions he wasn't ready to answer.

Yet he could admit that truth to himself, that he fancied her more than he'd ever fancied any other woman. In fact, he thought he might be on the verge of being in love with her. But he really couldn't ponder that with his mother standing right there, practically salivating over the prospect of his having a romantic interest.

"This is wonderful news! Although I will admit I never really thought that Lady Lily would be the woman to catch your eye, but I am glad she has. She is a sweet young woman."

"That she is, Mother. I should go fetch the carriage now." Before she could say anything else, thus making him trip over his tongue even more than he already had, he left the room and headed outside.

Lily had no idea if the pounding of her heart was caused by the excitement of knowing she was the "bait" for an established thief, or by the handsome man standing beside her. He hadn't left her side since she had arrived with her great Aunt Margaret, whom she had coerced into being her chaperone for the night. Aunt Margaret had quickly seated herself among the eldest party attendees, who fortunately were also her closest friends. They were seated in a semicircle in the corner of the drawing room, chatting away, no doubt discussing and dissecting the latest round of gossip circulating through the peerage. Lily had assumed the septuagenarian would not leave her seat for the rest of the night.

Lily gazed at the man on her arm. For the past few minutes they had been walking on the perimeter of the ballroom, the Ruby Key prominently displayed on her white-gloved right wrist, which was resting lightly in the crook of his arm. The jewels were beautifully offset by the darkness of his jacket and the delicate fabric of her glove. As they strode amidst the crowd, she tried to keep her focus on their mission, not on him. But it was exceedingly difficult not to simply gawk at him like a foolish schoolgirl experiencing her first crush.

Everything about him was perfect, from his expertly tied cravat to the high gloss of his dress shoes. He was devastatingly gorgeous. Adding to his appeal was his apparent obliviousness to his own appearance. The man simply didn't fathom how good-looking he truly was.

"How are you holding up?" he asked, halting their steps.

"Fine," she said, despite the butterflies tickling inside her stomach. He, however, seemed very calm. She tried to emulate his serenity. She glanced around the room, surveying the area. She watched as the throng of party-goers circulated and visited with each other. Each time her gaze landed on a man who was unfamiliar to her, she wondered if he was the thief. But to her untrained eye she couldn't discern if anyone was acting suspicious. Everyone seemed quite normal to her.

"Good," Colin said, redirecting her thoughts. They stood there for a moment, his gaze holding hers.

"What?" she finally asked after the silence between them stretched.

"It is just that . . . you look beautiful tonight, Lily."

Her mouth parted slightly in surprise. Had she heard him correctly? Did he really say she looked beautiful? She glanced down at her dress, a sage-colored satin gown with an emerald green ribbon tied at the empire waistline.

"You do," he said emphatically, as if he could read her thoughts. "You are the loveliest woman in the room."

"Now you are being ridiculous, Colin." The party was filled with lovely women, none of whom she could be compared to.

"No," he said, leaning close to her. "I am simply telling the truth."

A shiver traveled down her body as he whispered in her ear. She smiled, and he gave her a gleaming one in return.

"Ah, Lady Lily!" Michael approached them, his ever-present quizzing glass held at the usual perfect angle. "And Lord Chesreton. So nice to see both of you here." Michael extended his hand to Lily, who put her gloved one in his. As he leaned over it he whispered, "You were scrutinizing everyone a moment before. Stop being so obvious." Planting a soft kiss on the top of her fingers, he straightened, then peered at Colin through his glass. "I trust that everything is well with you?"

"Yes," Colin replied, tucking Lily's hand tightly into the crook of his arm. "Lady Lily and I plan on having an *uneventful* evening."

"Very well then, I shall leave you both to it. Have a pleasant time." Spinning smartly on one dress heel, he walked off. Lily watched him for a moment, astounded at the ease with which he mingled with the other guests while remaining on his guard. Her esteem of him kept climbing higher and higher, for he was very skilled at his profession.

The orchestra finished the current song, then immediately went into a minuet. The soft sounds of the violins wafted in the air around them. Colin turned to her. "Shall we dance, my lady?"

She smiled. "By all means, my lord."

Colin led her out on the floor, and they took their positions. He whirled her around the entire dance floor according to their plan, maximizing their exposure to the crowd. From their first step she was enthralled with the music and with the man whose hand was pressed firmly at the small of her back. Every nerve-ending felt alive. But soon it became apparent he wasn't focused on her, or on the dance at all.

"Sorry," he said after she tripped over his foot for the third time.

"What is wrong with you?" she whispered. One couple passed them by, giving them a questioning look. She responded with a tight smile. "Have you forgotten the dance?"

'No," he said, turning a corner and jerking her closer

to him with more force than she thought was necessary. "Perhaps I should remind you that the dance is not the reason we're here."

His words put quite the dent in her puffed-up mood. She frowned.

He glanced around her shoulder once more. "I am finding it exceedingly difficult to keep my attention on the crowd and on the dance."

"Colin, you do not have to try so hard. Michael has everything taken care of. Nothing is going to happen."

"I hope not." He turned his head to the side, then stepped on the toe of her slipper.

"Ouch," she said through gritted teeth.

"A thousand pardons." But he didn't sound all that sorry. In fact, he sounded most preoccupied. She hid a smile as she realized why he was so pensive. He was preoccupied with her welfare.

Her gaze went to the bracelet on her wrist, prominently displayed as he held her hand up while they danced. The sight of it sobered her completely. He was right to take this seriously. It was about time she did the same. As they continued to dance, she focused on showing off the bracelet, all while dodging his wayward steps.

The dance ended, and the room filled with the soft sound of gloved clapping. Several of the couples made their way off the floor toward the refreshment table, even as the orchestra began another song.

Lily waited to see if Colin would ask her to dance again. He had to be in a quandary over this. It would be another prime opportunity for her to show off the bracelet. But if he did request another dance, it would cement in everyone's minds that he had intentions regarding her. He had said he didn't care what anyone else thought about his attention to her, but dancing twice in a row was something else entirely. According to society rules, if he did that he might as well announce to the *ton* that they were betrothed.

Her face flushed at the thought. Her and Colin betrothed—what a wonderful idea. And a fanciful one, of course. She wished she could keep her mind from entertaining such thoughts, but with him standing right next to her, and telling her she looked beautiful, it was exceedingly difficult not to.

"Oh, Lord Chesreton!"

Lily turned to see Carolina Derry heading toward them. She tried to stem the ugly emotions beginning to bubble up in her. Carolina looked as elegant as ever, her peach-colored dress with a pearl-encrusted neckline perfectly complimenting her creamy skin and reddish blond hair.

"There you are, my lord," Carolina said when she reached them. "I have been looking all over for you. We have not had our customary evening dance."

"Miss Derry, I am afraid I cannot—"

"Now, now, Colin, there is no reason why you cannot dance with me right now." She looked directly at Lily. "At least none I can see."

"Miss Derry," Colin said, his tone shifting from polite to stern. "As you can see, I already have a partner."

Carolina reached out and boldly grasped Colin's arm. "Come now, Lord Chesreton. I believe you have done enough charity work for the evening." She tugged on his sleeve.

Lily watched with bemusement at the woman's desperate attempts to get Colin to dance with her. In fact she was so insistent Lily assumed he would acquiesce. It was either that or risk making a scene, as Carolina firmly had him in her clutches. It was quite sad, really, and for once Lily felt something other than jealousy in the woman's presence. She actually felt pity. "Colin," she said. "It is all—"

Colin steadied himself and retracted his arm from Carolina's hand. "Miss Derry, stop, please. I will not dance with you. Not tonight, nor any other night."

Chapter Twenty-one

Colin's conscience lurched at the sight of Carolina Derry's shocked and stricken expression. But he didn't feel too guilty. After all, she had given him no other choice. It was quite bold and rude of her to assume he would abandon Lily just to dance with her. He also didn't appreciate her tactics. It made her appear desperate, a quality he found most unattractive.

Besides, he wasn't about to leave Lily's side, not for anything, and especially not for Carolina Derry.

"How dare you," Carolina said. She glanced around to see if anyone had noticed his overt rejection of her, visibly breathing a sigh of relief when she saw everyone else attending to their own party business. Still, she obviously wasn't about to let it go. Moving closer to him, she lowered her voice. "How dare you humiliate me like that?"

"I beg your pardon, Carolina," he said. "It was not my intention to embarrass you, I can assure you."

Her toxic expression immediately lifted, replaced by a flirtatious glow. The ease with which she could switch moods was quite dizzying. And extremely off-putting, in his opinion. "I accept your apology," she said brightly, attempting to loop her arm in his. "Now, we shall dance." She pulled him aside, a few steps away from Lily.

"No, I am afraid you misunderstand me. I am sorry if I embarrassed you, but I still won't dance with you. As I stated before, I am with someone else."

"Lily?" Carolina scoffed. "Please. I cannot believe you are with *her*."

"Why not?" His gaze bore into hers.

Carolina laughed. "Well, look at her for one thing. She is hardly prime now, is she?"

Her ill opinion of Lily got under his skin. "I have looked at her, quite often as a matter of fact." He enjoyed watching Carolina's superior expression slide off her face. "And I find her prime. Very prime indeed."

"You cannot be serious, Colin. Someone like you with someone like . . . her? It does not happen that way. Beautiful people are paired with other beautiful people. That is how it has always been."

"Beauty is in the eye of the beholder, Carolina. And speaking of beauty, what will you do when yours fades? Because it surely will, someday. When that happens, will you have anything left? You should think about that."

"How . . . how . . . dare you!" she spouted. Her plump lips pursed into a pout. "Colin Dymoke, you are a perfectly horrid man. I cannot believe I ever saw a future for us!"

"That, Miss Derry, is something you and I can both agree on."

"Oh!" She whirled around in a cloud of peach and pearl and stormed off, presumably in search of Evelyn Derry. He could only imagine the diatribe she would expel to her mother and anyone else who was listening. But he didn't care. Perhaps he hadn't handled that in the most delicate manner, but he had gotten his point across. Carolina had it coming to her, that much was for sure. He was grateful Lily hadn't been close enough to hear the conversation.

He turned to look for her, but she was nowhere in sight. His gut clenched. Panicked, he searched the ballroom. Something was wrong, he just knew it inside. Something was terribly, horribly wrong.

Chapter Twenty-two

Lily didn't know how it happened. One minute she was standing next to Colin and Carolina, the next she had been swept onto the dance floor by none other than George Clayburn.

"Brings back old times, does it not, Lady Lily?" He jerked and whirled her around, leading her to the center of the dance floor. His movements were harsh and completely lacking in grace. She remembered he had never been the greatest of dancers.

"I do not want to dance with you," she hissed. "It is most boorish for you to assume that I would."

"Now, now, Lady Lily," George said. "You wouldn't want to make a scene, would you?"

Whatever his purpose in asking her to dance, he couldn't have picked a worse time. She tried to search the ballroom for Colin, but George tilted his head to block her view.

"Looking for Lord Chesreton? Whatever for?"

"We were planning to dance," she pointed out, albeit with a touch of uncertainty.

"I find that hard to believe. Besides, I just saw him speaking with Carolina Derry. He appeared very interested in *her*."

Lily's lips flattened into a thin line. "Unhand me this instant!"

Instead of complying he tightened his grip on her hand, squeezing her fingers together until they ached. "I do not believe I will. I am certainly under no obligation to agree to your demands. Not anymore."

"I never demanded anything of you!"

"Didn't you? Didn't you insist on complete loyalty? Total monogamy? Most unfair of you, I must say."

Anger flared within her as he continued to turn her around in small circles, never leaving the center of the ballroom floor. They were surrounded by couples; indeed, the dance floor seemed crammed with them. Even she could easily be lost in the mass. "You would have cheated on me with half the women in the *ton,* George. I have far more pride—and standards—than to put up with that. The best thing I ever did was to get rid of you."

His mouth upturned into an ugly smile. "But, my lady, I am still very much here." His gaze went to her wrist. "What a lovely bracelet," he said, not sounding the least bit sincere. "Is it new?"

"Yes," she said, her voice suddenly shaking. No

longer was he looking at her, but at the dazzling jewels. Why the sudden interest?

"Who gave it to you?"

"Colin," she blurted, unable to think clearly.

George's black brows rose. "Quite an extravagance," he said, still looking at the bracelet. He inclined his head closer to her wrist. "Where did he purchase it?"

"How should I know?" she replied hotly. "It was a gift. It would be bad form to question where he purchased it."

"If indeed he did purchase it," George mumbled. He swirled her around again, peering over her shoulder. Then inexplicably he stumbled over his feet, causing Lily to ram right into him.

"George, this ridiculousness has gone on long enough. Let me go."

He ignored her, continuing to look over her shoulder. She turned around to find out what he was looking at. Instantly she saw Colin, still speaking with Carolina, who looked quite upset. Lily tilted her head and tried to get his attention, hoping he would see her and save her from this insufferable man.

Yet before she could turn back around George swept her in his arms, both dancing and dragging her to the opposite side of the room. Before she realized what was happening he had led her out of the room and into a long corridor.

She planted her feet on the wood floor and forced him to halt. "What do you think you are doing?" she said, trying to twist her hand out of his grip.

"What I should have done a long time ago." His voice was fierce and low.

A shiver of true fear ran down her spine at his black tone. Even though they had been at odds for a long while, he had never spoken to her with such poisonous hate. "George—"

"Shut up!" He grabbed her wrist tightly. "Say one more word and you will be dead."

Stark fear gripped Colin, unlike any he'd ever experienced before. He dashed through the crowd on the perimeter of the room. He ignored the strange looks the partygoers cast in his direction as he searched for Michael. Blast the man. He was nowhere to be seen. Confound it, any other time he made sure his presence was known.

Colin called himself every kind of fool and idiot for letting Carolina distract him. For all he knew she was in cahoots with the burglar and her display was a ruse to keep him from protecting Lily. It seemed more than a coincidence that she showed up and separated him from Lily, only to have Lily disappear a short moment later. Perhaps she had laid a trap for him, and like a knucklehead he had walked right into it.

Then suddenly he caught a glimpse of Lily's back as she was dragged into a hallway by someone he couldn't see. He rushed to follow her, only to be blocked by Clewes, who walked right in front of him.

"Move," Colin hissed, craning his neck around the

thin man. He had to keep his eye on Lily. She was in danger. He sensed it—no, he *knew* it. His heart pounded in his chest, and if Clewes didn't move right that instant, he would knock the man out himself.

"Calm down, my lord," Clewes said, his tone and demeanor the picture of serenity. "You cannot let your emotions get the best of you."

"But Lily—"

"We know, my lord." Clewes pretended to brush a stray piece of lint off his jacket. "Lord Hathery knows exactly where she is. And once you have gathered your wits about you, I will take you to her."

Colin nodded, taking a deep breath. The man was right, he couldn't go after Lily half cocked. Any reckless behavior would put her in more serious danger.

Threads of acute pain shot up Lily's forearm, but she remained silent. She believed George's threat, as he had said it with chilling sincerity. He continued to pull her along the length of the hallway and farther into the house. When he reached the end he pushed on a heavy oak door, which led to the outside garden. When they were in the center of the garden, he held up her wrist and whipped off the decoy bracelet.

"No," she cried as he slipped the jewelry in his pocket. "How dare you take that from me?"

George scoffed. "Spare me your dramatic overtures, Lily. I dare to take it because I can. And there is nothing you can do to stop me."

His hand clung fast to her wrist, nearly blinding her with pain. "Please . . . let me go."

"Not yet, my sweet. I rather enjoying seeing you like this, at my mercy. Do you have any idea how you have humiliated me in the months since you cast me off?"

"Humiliated you? It most certainly was the other way around. How do you think that made me feel, knowing you were with other women while engaged to me?"

"I could not care less about your feelings," George said. "I thought you knew that. You should have been grateful that I took an interest in you, Lily, when no one else would."

"Stop it." She tried to pull away from him, but he held on to her harder. "Why are you doing this to me?"

"Because I can. You have denied me the status and money I deserve, Lily. I could have been the son-in-law of a duke, with all the power and prestige affording the title. I could have had it all, you know, instead of scraping by, barely staying out of debtors prison. All I had to do was marry a wealthy, naive, *desperate* woman. You, *love*, fit that description exactly.

"Then you broke our engagement. You embarrassed me in front of the peerage and denied me what I worked so hard to earn. Can you imagine trying to explain why the likes of you dissolved our betrothal? It was as if you thought you were too good for *me*."

"I am," she insisted, smearing the tears off her cheek. She would not allow him to wound her with his verbal daggers. *You look beautiful.* Colin's words resonated in her mind, deflecting the painful words

George had spewed at her. "Your shenanigans tonight only prove it. Now let me go, before I make a scene that will be heard from here to Leeds."

"I doubt that will happen." He thrust his hand into the inside pocket of his jacket and pulled out a handful of bejeweled bracelets. "Well, what do we have here?"

Lily's eyes grew wide. "You are the bandit," she said, barely able to believe it.

"How deductive of you," he said snidely. "Although I'm surprised it took you this long to figure it out. It was quite easy to cast suspicion on you while I continued to search for the real treasure. Planting that bracelet in your cloak was child's play. Oh, it is simply amazing the total falsehoods a gossip columnist will write about if they sound like they have a grain of truth in them. Thanks to you, I now have the Key. And once I sell it I will have more money than even you can dream of."

Lily breathed an inward sigh of relief. From what she could tell George had no idea the bracelet was fake. He was so far off track as to be laughable, considering the Key not only wasn't a gift from Colin, is was totally counterfeit. Then an idea occurred to her. If she could keep him out here talking long enough, Colin and Michael would surely know she was missing. She had to allow them enough time to find her.

"I suppose I should give you a dash of gratitude," he continued. "If you had not rejected me I would not have learned about the Ruby Key and its value among the more nefarious characters of humanity. You would not believe how much money some of these countries will pay for British secrets." He chuckled mirthlessly. "And to think such a valuable trinket was a gift from Lord Chesreton. I doubt he knows its true value, though. Well, it does not matter, because in a few moments the man will have nothing to do with you, not after you have been branded a thief."

"That won't happen," Lily cried. "I have not stolen anything. And despite your efforts, no one else believes I have."

"But they will when you are caught red-handed." He thrust the bracelets into her hand and closed her fist around them. Dragging her through the garden and closer to the house, he started to shout. "I found her! I found the Bracelet Bandit!"

Chapter Twenty-three

"Why aren't we doing anything?" Colin snapped at Michael from their hiding place in the Mantuas' garden. They could easily hear George Clayburn's loud accusation regarding Lily and the bracelets. In fact, his booming voice echoed throughout the small garden. It was only a matter of time before someone inside the house got wind of what was going on outside.

Michael remained silent and still. Colin wanted to throttle the man. It was Michael's fault Lily was in this precarious position, and Colin believed he should have never let Lily get involved in this stupid plan. His worst fears had come to fruition—Lily was in trouble. When Clewes had brought Colin out here, Michael had impassively told him that it was George who had abducted Lily, and the cretin was more than likely the Bracelet

Bandit. But since then Michael hadn't said a word or made a move.

Colin, however, couldn't wait any longer. They were crouched behind a row of fragrant rosebushes, their sweet aroma mixing with the panic in his gut and making his stomach roll. "Blast it, Michael. If you won't help her, I will."

"Colin," Michael said, his voice low and filled with warning. "Shut up and stay put. Now isn't the time."

"And when will that be? When half the *ton* believes her a thief? Or when George does something even more despicable to her?" When Michael didn't acknowledge him, Colin shot up from his position and stormed off in the direction of George's voice. He would have to handle this himself.

"I have caught her red-handed!" George continued to shout. "*The Daily Chronicle* was right after all—Lily Breckenridge is a thief!"

Colin emerged into the courtyard of the garden to see George gripping Lily's hand, which was formed into a fist. By the expression on her face and the angle at which her arm was bent he could tell she was in acute pain. Rage exploded inside him. "Unhand her," he yelled as he barreled toward Clayburn. "Now!"

"Colin," Lily said weakly. Her brown eyes caught his for a moment, and he detected the relief in them. Her need for him bolstered his resolve.

George's head whipped around at the sound of Colin's voice. "What ho, look what we have here." He laughed, but didn't let go of Lily. Instead he squeezed her fist even tighter, causing her to cry out in pain.

"George, please . . . you are hurting me."

"I am?" He looked at her, a sinister grin forming on his thin lips. *"Good."*

"Clayburn, I am warning you . . ." Colin clenched his fists and took a step forward.

"Oh, now that is rich. You warning me? With what exactly? Let me guess, you plan to overpower me. You probably could, or at least give me a good run. However, I do not plan to let it get that far." His free hand delved into his pocket. A metal blade appeared, glinting in the moonlight. George drew Lily to him, placing the knife against her throat. "Now, I suggest you remain in your place, Lord Chesreton. For if you take one more step forward, I will plunge this steel into her throat."

Cold terror shot through Colin at the sight of the blade tip against her delicate skin. "You are bluffing," he said, albeit weakly.

"Pity you do not gamble, my lord, for if you did you would know that I never bluff." He moved his mouth close to Lily's ears. "So this is your knight in shining armor? It seems he is truly concerned for your welfare. Imagine that."

Fury unlike any Colin had experienced before unleashed within him. He was equally angry with himself as much as Clayburn. He should have listened to Michael, instead of letting his emotions get the best of him. Bitter irony welled inside him as he remembered how annoyed he always was with Lily when she acted impulsively. But she had never put him in any danger. However, his own recklessness could get her killed.

"Clayburn. Why do not we talk about this," he said, deliberately using a conciliatory tone. He glanced at Lily. Stark fear shone in her eyes, but she still managed to hold herself together. Another woman with less inner strength might have liquefied into hysterics by now. But not his Lily.

George smirked. "He is getting desperate, my lady," he said to Lily. "Look at him. He is nearly at the point of begging. If I did not know any better, I would say he fancies you." At Colin's flinch, George's black eyebrows raised. "Well now, that elicited a reaction, did it not? Perhaps Lord Chesreton has deep feelings for you, Lily. Perhaps the man even loves you." George looked directly at Colin, his voice caustic and harsh. "Is that true, my lord? Do you love our *fair* Lady Lily?"

Colin gulped. What was this man trying to do? Bait him? But for what reason? His gaze met Lily's questioning one. She too wanted an answer; he could see it in her eyes. They were both waiting for him to reply. He could do nothing but tell them the truth.

Black spots swam before Lily's eyes. It took every bit of courage she had to keep from fainting dead away. She couldn't feel her left hand anymore, as George had not eased his grip on her one whit. Fortunately it kept her from feeling the jewels of the bracelets cutting through her glove and into the flesh of her palm. But that was the only good thing. The cold steel of the blade point remained at her throat, and every few seconds George pressed it against her, a reminder that he held her life in his hands.

And there was Colin, standing before her, helpless and looking extremely confused. Lily couldn't believe that with her life in such dire straights, with that madman George holding her hostage, all she could think about was what Colin's answer to George's question would be. It was ridiculously insecure of her, but she couldn't help herself.

Then their gazes met and locked. And suddenly she knew. She didn't have to hear the words. She could see the emotion in his eyes. She felt it in her heart.

"Yes," he said softly, his eyes not leaving her. "I love her."

"Oh, Colin," she said.

"Oh, Colin," George mimicked. He rolled his eyes. "I suppose your father has promised him your huge dowry. A dowry that was meant for me, as a matter of fact."

"Colin does not need my money. His family is wealthy enough."

"Tsk, tsk. My lady sounds defensive." George aimed his next words at Colin. "Perhaps because she suspects your words are false, as do I. Perhaps she knows what I do—you do not love her. You pity her. Just like everyone else does."

"Enough of your games, Clayburn," Colin said. "Let her go—"

Lily drew in a sharp intake of breath as the blade dug into her skin. Colin blanched, taking a step back.

"I am in charge here," George said, suddenly very, very serious. "You need remember that. All my life I have taken orders from other people. Done their bidding. Kowtowed to their desires. No longer. Once I have sold the Ruby Key, I will control my own destiny." He glowered at Lily. "I will have a much better life than I would have spent pretending to love you."

"I think not."

George froze as the barrel of a gun touched his temple. Michael had snuck up behind them with such stealth none of them had heard him. He moved from the shadows and stepped to the side, the gun still aimed at George's head.

"Drop the knife and release Lady Lily. Now."

The blade hit the ground with a thud. At the same time he let go of Lily's hand, the bracelets falling on the cobblestone path, the jewels making tiny clinking sounds as they hit the hard stones. Lily immediately ran to Colin, who enfolded her in his arms.

"Are you all right, love?" he asked, holding her close.

Love. The word sounded so good, so right coming from him. She nodded, leaning her cheek against his shoulder.

"I-I can explain," George stammered, moving to face Michael. "This is not what it looks like."

Cocking the hammer of the pistol, Michael replied, "Stand down, Mr. Clayburn. Your explanations are of no interest to me. Clewes." Michael summoned the man, who seemed to appear out of thin air. Two broad-shouldered men flanked him. "Take care of Mr. Clayburn." The largest man jerked George's hands behind his back and held them there.

Michael pocketed his pistol once George was in custody. "Make sure he gets exactly what he deserves," he ordered.

"Yes, my lord." With a short bow Clewes, George, and the other two men departed, George still proclaiming his innocence until his desperate cries disappeared into the night air.

Lily melted against Colin, her body drawing in his warmth, allowing her hammering heartbeat to slow down. Her senses reeled as he rubbed her back, his hand coming up and reaching to rest on the back of her neck.

"Are you certain you are all right?" Colin asked.

"Yes," she said. "I am. But I was so frightened, Colin. So very frightened."

"I couldn't tell. You were brave in the extreme." He paused. "I am so sorry," he whispered to her. "I should have never let you do this—"

"Colin—"

"I should not have allowed myself to become distracted. This never would have happened if I had kept my promise—"

"Colin—"

"Lily—"

"Colin!" She stepped back to search his face. "Listen

to me. It is over. It is finally over. Berating yourself over this serves no purpose."

"But it was my fault."

"Hardly. You are not to blame for George being a thief, or for his hatred toward me." Her lips tilted in a half smile. "Believe it or not, the world does not revolve around you, Colin Dymoke."

His tortured expression faded, then dissolved into a smile. His hand cupped her cheek, and he brushed his thumb across her cheekbone. "Amazing. Here you are comforting me after what you just went through."

"Of all the foolhardy, lamebrained, pickle-headed things to do," Michael muttered.

Lily turned in Colin's arms, but didn't step out of his embrace as Michael stormed toward them. She suppressed a smile, for the earl sounded quite a bit like Emily when she was upset.

Michael's green eyes practically glowed with anger. He aimed his ire directly at Colin. "We had everything under control, Dymoke."

"I know," Colin responded.

"Do not ever, ever, *ever* ignore a direct order from me again. Is that clear?"

"Um, yes." Colin frowned at Michael's directive. "What do you mean *again*?"

Michael quirked a brow, his ire diminishing somewhat. "Nothing. Nothing at all." He fussed with his waistcoat, brushed his lapels, and retrieved his quizzing glass from the pocket of his jacket. "Just remember, one never knows what the future holds." Leaning forward, he grasped Lily's hand and brushed a kiss along the gloved knuckles. "It has been a pleasure working with you, my lady." He straightened. "Thank you for your help."

Colin and Lily watched as he walked away, leaving them alone in the garden. She stepped out of his embrace. She tried to process everything that had happened. "I still cannot believe George was the thief."

"I cannot believe he had the brains to pull off such a scheme."

Lily smiled, but it faded quickly. "And to think . . . I nearly married him. If I had not caught him with the maid and broke off our engagement . . ." she shuddered.

"Shh . . . ," Colin said, moving toward her. "Do not think about that. It did not happen, so you mustn't dwell on it."

"You are right, of course. We should concentrate on the present." She cast a glance around the garden. "So this is it? The English government was on the brink of collapse, I was on the verge of death . . . and everything goes back to normal?"

Colin shrugged. "Apparently so. I do not really understand how these spy things are supposed to work out. It is my first time, you know." He grinned.

"Well, then. What do we do now?" Lily stretched out the fingers of her cramped hand. The pain had lessened, and a quick glance at her glove showed that the stones hadn't drawn blood. Everything truly was back to normal.

The faint strains of music wafted on the light breeze filtering through the garden air. Colin grasped Lily's hand. "We dance."

"Dance?" Lily took a step away, then turned her back on Colin. A sudden surge of doubt plagued her. Every word, every ugly mocking word George spoke came rushing back to her. Colin had said he loved her, but did he really? Or was George right—did Colin simply pity her?

She couldn't bear it if he did.

"Lily?" Colin came up behind her, placing his hands on her shoulders. "What is it?"

"It is . . ." She felt like an insecure ninny, because that's exactly what she was. Her mind couldn't accept what her heart wanted so desperately—for Colin Dymoke to love her.

His hands slowly slid from her shoulders down her arms, causing a shiver to course through her. She couldn't stop a sigh from escaping as he wrapped his arms around her waist, pulled her against him and rested his chin against her shoulder. "George is gone," he said softly. "He cannot hurt you anymore."

"It is not that."

"Then what is it?" He pressed his lips against her ear. "Tell me, love. Tell me what is wrong."

She took a deep breath. "I am being silly."

"You are never silly, Lily. Impulsive, yes. But not silly. And that is one of the things I love about you." He spun her around in his arms until they were face to face. "One of the many things, I might add."

She searched his face. "You really do, don't you?"

He questioned her with a lift of his brow.

"Love me." Her breath caught as she waited for his reply.

He smiled. "Yes. I am just sorry it took me so long to realize it."

"Colin, we have only known each other a few weeks."

"Exactly my point. What took me so long?"

"Colin, I am being serious."

"As am I. I love you, Lily."

"But are you sure?"

"Botheration, woman, you can suck the romance right out of a moment, cannot you?" He stilled, his expression growing somber. "I know I have not been sure about a lot of things, Lily. And it must seem to you that I do not know my own mind half the time. I am hoping to rectify that starting now. But if there is one thing I am sure of it is my love for you."

She blinked back the tears. "Oh, Colin. I love you too, so very much."

His gaze dropped to her mouth. Tilting his head, he captured her lips with his own, kissing her gently, but with exquisite emotion. She returned his kiss, sighing deeply.

"There," he said when they parted. "Now that we are both on the same page, we should probably return to the party before we are missed."

"I suppose we should." But her feet refused to move. Instead she brushed back the lock of blond hair touching his forehead. "We should leave right away."

"Yes." He continued to gaze at her, his head inclining toward hers once more. "Straight away." He kissed her again, this time longer and more thoroughly.

"We really must leave," he said, stepping back from her and sounding a little breathless. "Seriously. Now is not the time to ruin your reputation. Not when we have gone to such great lengths to save it."

"I suppose you are right."

They walked, arm in arm, through the back door of the house, down the long corridor George had dragged her through, and entered the ballroom. The musicians were still playing, the couples still dancing, the women and men still gossiping. It was as if they had never been gone.

Colin grinned, then looked at Lily. "Shall we dance?"

Her smile was her answer.

He swept her onto the dance floor, holding her more tightly than he had ever done before, in public anyway. She was acutely aware of the curious glances of the other dancers, but she didn't care. Everyone would know soon enough that Colin Dymoke had intentions where Lady Lily was concerned. Very serious intentions.

They danced the next song as well, nearly bumping into Emily and Michael as the couple stiffly moved about the ballroom floor. Lily and Colin watched them for a moment. Michael appeared as self-absorbed as ever. And for once Emily didn't look miserable in his arms, only resigned.

"They make a rather striking couple do not you think?" Lily asked as they twirled around the dance floor.

Colin's brow lifted. "Michael and Emily?" He studied them for a moment, as if considering agreeing with her. Then he shook his head. "No. She despises him."

"But she does not really know him." Lily continued to watch the couple as they danced. "Apparently no one truly does."

"He wants to keep it that way, Lily."

"I know, but . . ."

"Oh, bother."

"What?" Lily looked back at Colin, who had a pseudo-annoyed expression on his face.

"No matchmaking."

"But maybe I can help."

"No, Lily. I insist upon it."

"You insist?" she huffed.

"Yes. You will be too busy, to concern yourself with anyone else's relationship, anyway." He leaned forward and whispered in her ear. "Now that I have you, I want your undivided attention."

She laughed. "Is that an order?"

"Let's call it a sincere request."

Smiling, she leaned against him, and gave him exactly what he wanted.